Seductively

Debra Kayn

author of Breathing His Air and Wildly

CRIMSON
ROMANCE
F+W Media, Inc.

This edition published by
Crimson Romance
an imprint of F+W Media, Inc.
10151 Carver Road, Suite 200
Blue Ash, Ohio 45242
www.crimsonromance.com

ISBN 10: 1-4405-6649-6
ISBN 13: 978-1-4405-6649-3
eISBN 10: 1-4405-6650-X
eISBN 13: 978-1-4405-6650-9

Wheels—After all these years, we finally have our "thing." Other people have their song, their anniversary, their moment that they share together. We have our thing. I love our thing. No one else can have our thing.

Chapter One

If Stan Dogger raised his voice any louder, Diana Spenner was going to scream. It was bad enough he decided to call her out on her last hour of working before her two weeks of vacation started, but she had no desire to tell the hotel owner the real reason she wanted to continue working and skip her down time.

Except she had a little thing called a temper, and Mr. Dogger had used his quota of bossiness for the day. She clamped her lips. *Let it go, let it go…*

"You're going to die of a heart attack if you keep working every day without a break." Mr. Dogger fisted his hands on his waist.

Oh, now he was just being ridiculous. "I'm twenty-four. I'm not going to keel over because I like working a forty-hour week. Besides, I already promised I'd take a couple of weeks off in the spring, before tourist season starts." She smiled extra wide, hoping against the odds he'd change his mind.

"That's six months away," he said.

"Come on, Mr. Dogger." She lowered her voice and stepped closer. "Admit it. You need me here. You don't want to cover for me. Mrs. Dogger wants to take you to Napa Valley for a week. It'd be the perfect time to get away, enjoy the sunshine, drink some wine, and buy your wife those fancy red heels she's eyed at Sallie's Shoes."

His bushy gray brows lowered. "I've known you since you were a little girl. Don't be using my wife against me. If I hear you've conspired behind my back with Adele, I'll fire you. Now, go home!"

She scoffed. "Fine. I expect you to call me if things get too hectic. I'll even fill in for one of the servers in the lounge if anyone calls in sick."

As the hotel manager, she usually oversaw the front desk, scheduled the other employees, and made sure the guests were enjoying their stay without any complaints. But, she wasn't going to turn down extra work if she could convince Mr. Dogger to fit her in elsewhere at the hotel. With tourist season upon them, he could use the extra help.

"Get out of here." He pointed to the doorway. "Go. Not another word."

Discouraged, she gathered her laptop and fled the office. She'd counted on working the extra hours and taking her vacation pay at the same time. The money from earning double time wages would've set her a month ahead of schedule on her dream of purchasing the old Ferriday place. That'd move her next goal of opening a bed and breakfast up to next summer. Now she was going to have to wait until December to purchase the house, and hope that no one bought it in the meantime.

Of course, she couldn't tell Mr. Dogger why she wanted to work. Soon, she'd be his only competition in the small valley. The less people knew of her plans, the better.

She wasn't going to let anyone talk her out of doing what she wanted. One word about her decision to spend her savings, and her parents would do whatever they could to discourage her. That's why she'd deposited her money at the Cottage Grove Credit Union, and not her father's bank across the street. She even refused to mention a word about her dreams to her best friends, Shauna and Kate, and she usually never kept anything secret from them.

A woman's loud scream came from behind her. She whirled around and barely jumped out of the way of three women running toward the lobby. Clutching her laptop to her chest, she gazed after them. Something exciting must have happened in the otherwise quiet town.

She followed them at a slower pace, arriving in the front of the hotel to find a packed room. She studied the area, and frowned. It seemed every woman staying at the hotel had gathered in front of her.

The last time she saw this big of a crowd was during the Cottage Grove Fundraiser two months ago when Dominic Chekovsky, a professional hockey player, made an appearance in public. The hair at the back of her neck moved as another woman ran past her to enter the large group congregating in front of the double glass doors. She shivered as a bad feeling came over her, one Shauna would say was a cosmic sign from Jupiter that a major roadblock was headed her way.

Silence swept through the crowd, and the cluster of women parted in what she'd call quiet reverence. She squinted, peering around the shoulders of the women. A ball of foreboding settled under her ribs, followed by a gasp. She refused to call her reaction an adrenaline rush or an attraction that threatened to careen out of control.

She'd barely accepted the reality of seeing the biggest pain in her ass when Dominic Chekovsky strolled across the blue carpet in all his six foot four glory, straight toward her. His blond hair short and swept to the side framed a face women could only call stunning. The angled cheeks, dominant chin, all atop broad shoulders, slim waist, and thick thighs. He really was a nicely sculpted man, until he opened his mouth.

His eyes so light blue, they appeared more ice-like, gave him an intense gaze. A gaze he directed straight at her.

She stood straighter and lifted her chin. A week ago, she'd punched him in the stomach when he wouldn't move out of her way and accept she wasn't interested in dating him. This time, if he refused to take no for an answer, she'd hit him over his hard head with her laptop. Then sue him for damages. She had no interest in dating a professional athlete. Especially one with an ego bigger than the stadium or coliseum or whatever kind of building hockey players played in.

She'd witnessed how women reacted to him. She would never lower herself to scream and claw over anyone, no matter how sexy he was in person.

"Diana. It's so good to see you again." Dominic stopped in front of her.

"What are you doing here?" She stepped back when the women pressed in on all sides of her.

"I must talk with you." He ignored the other women. "Maybe somewhere we can be alone without an audience. Please?"

His Russian accent was thick, each word pronounced with emphasis as if he meant to hold his audience captive. She glanced around and rolled her eyes. Each woman crowded around him held their breath, waiting for him to give them each a bit of personal attention.

"It's important, Diana," he said.

"I don't believe you." She waved her hand dismissively. "Take your pick, stud. Any one of them would love to spend time with you and listen to what you have to say."

The crowd vibrated with tension. She fought the urge to tell them all to get a life. It was utterly ridiculous seeing grown women, most of them married, throwing themselves in Dominic's path.

"Shauna told me to tell you it was in your best interest to talk with me." Dominic inched forward.

She groaned. He knew using Shauna, who'd do anything for Diana, as a pawn would work. Damn him.

Mr. Dogger was going to throw a fit when he hears about the disturbance Dominic was causing in the hotel again. He still hadn't forgiven Dominic for the damage the women caused last time he came to town. Although, the extra money Dominic gave

Mr. Dogger for the damage the women caused in their attempt to get to him ended up providing new tables in the lounge.

If Diana took him upstairs to her room at the hotel, the women would follow and never leave the vicinity. She caught her bottom lip between her teeth. Mr. Dogger would have no other option than to have her continue working after he realized the women would not leave as long as Dominic was here.

"Fine. You can come with me up to my room. Ten minutes. And you're not allowed to ask me out on a date." She pushed her way through the crowd, letting Dominic find his own way of keeping up with her.

In the elevator, she held her laptop in front of her body as a shield and kept the women from following them inside. Dominic squeezed past her. The doors slid closed, and she pushed the button, sending them up to the next floor, and relaxed.

"Thanks." Dominic leaned against the wall.

She watched the floor lights climb above the door. "Just so you know, I didn't do this for you. It's for Shauna."

"You wound me."

"You'll survive." She watched the lights climb above the doors. "This is my floor."

He followed her out of the elevator and down the hall. She shifted the laptop under her arm, and felt Dominic take it from her grasp. Without arguing over being perfectly fine managing on her own, she dug the key out of her pocket.

Most hotels upgraded to card keys years ago, but Mr. Dogger kept the old hotel to the original construction since he bought the place back in the seventies. She was lucky enough to convince him to change over to using computers six months ago to make her job easier.

The elevator pinged the second she swung the door open and the giggles from the women following them pushed her into action. She shoved Dominic inside before locking the door. The rumors of women, all women, being highly attracted to the star were no exaggeration. She'd seen the mobs that followed him, touched him without permission, and how the females threw themselves on him at the fundraiser. Later when she'd hung out with her friends at the Quayside, Dominic had to leave early because the women were causing a scene.

A small part of her could almost feel sorry for him. She took her laptop from him, set it on the table, and crossed her arms. "Okay, you've got ten minutes to say what you think is so important you had to interrupt my perfectly fine day."

She rarely invited anyone into her private room. Despite living in a hotel, she'd made the place her own. Plants lined the floor near the patio sliding door leading to the balcony. She'd bought fabric and covered the couch and chair with a floral print to brighten the room, and placed a few large wicker baskets around the sparse area that held her personal belongings. She might live in a hotel, but she needed her books, her CD's, and her sketchbook of the plans she was drawing.

She tilted her head and studied him. "Well? Are you going to tell me why you came to see me?"

Dominic's brow wrinkled and he stared at her before catching himself and walking across the room to peer out of the window. She waited. Her experience with Dominic usually caused her to become defensive, and him to lay everything out on the line.

Ever since he'd come to Cottage Grove—at her friend Shauna and her boyfriend, Grayson Schyler's request—he'd set out to sweep Diana off her feet. He was dominating and bossy, and no matter how many times she explained she wasn't interested in going out on a date, he became more determined to get her to change her mind. She had no idea how to get through to him.

She was not interested in dating him. Brent Thiegher, her college boyfriend, acted the same way. She'd dated him for over a year, despite knowing he was a flirt. All she saw was a star quarterback, sexy, popular, and smooth talker. One month after she broke up with him, knowing she'd never be happy in a relationship with him, she found out he'd seen three other women while they were supposed to be exclusive.

She eyed Dominic. He was a pro hockey player, sexy, popular, and a smooth talker too. Normally he had no problems bossing his way into a conversation. Today, his quietness unsettled her. Where was the charm? The flirting? The massive dose of self-confidence?

She moved over and sat on the edge of the couch. The subdued attitude bothered her. Something must've happened to —

She jumped to her feet. "Oh my God, is Shauna okay?"

He turned around. "Of course. I'm staying at Grayson's house. I saw her this morning before she went to work."

She sat back down. "And Grayson is okay too?"

"He's fine." Dominic walked across the room and sat on the other end of the couch, well away from her.

"Why are you back?" She gripped the cushion underneath her, knowing she sounded bitchy but unable to stop. Dominic needed no encouragement from her, or he'd assume she'd changed her mind about him. He'd be wrong.

She had no desire to go out with him. None. Ever. Not even if he begged. Okay, she might like to see him on his knees. Maybe then the women would stop throwing themselves at him if they saw a little humbleness thrown in with his huge ego.

She inhaled, catching a hint of spicy cologne. Her stomach fluttered, and she shook her head to snap out of finding him attractive. "Are you going to answer my question?"

He leaned forward and planted his elbows on his knees. "I need your help."

He joked. Her burst of laughter dwindled, until she frowned. This man had everything going for him. Fame, skills, wealth, and not to mention any woman he wanted at his fingertips. Why would he need her help?

All he had to do was ask people, and anyone would help him. He was famous. He even had a security team he usually took with him when out in public who helped him keep his distance from all the women who ran after him. She'd seen him handle himself just fine when he was around his friends.

"Come on, Dominic, talk. You're taking up my vacation time." She crossed her legs.

"Has anyone told you that you're pushy?

"All the time." She shrugged. "Why?"

"It's very attractive."

She snorted. "The answer's no."

"You don't know what I was going to ask you," he said.

"Let's see…" She swung her foot back and forth. "You're going to ask me out. That's what you do every time you see me, and my answer is still no."

He sighed and sat back, staring straight ahead and not looking at her. She studied his profile. His jaw twitched and he ran his hands along the length of his thighs. She gulped. Long, hard, thick thighs a woman could dig her nails into.

"Hockey season has started and I'd like you to come and stay with me at my place," he spoke quietly.

She shook her head in surprise. "So you're skipping dating and going straight to sex. The answer's still no. You do nothing for me."

God, she was a liar. He could do a lot for her, but thinking about *it* was different than actually doing *it*.

"Please." He shifted and faced her. "The women are affecting my playing. I have a company who keeps trying to steal my towels. I can't even sleep at night, because the coach said I have to make them all go away. I don't know how. You're the only one who can't stand me."

"Why do you think I can help you or I'd want to help? I don't even like you because you think everyone wants you."

"They do." His brows lowered and he sighed.

She shook her head. "That's why you irritate me."

"I have a proposition for you. I want you to pretend to be my girlfriend. Maybe you'll scare the women away. They're the source of my problem. They won't leave me alone. Day and night, they're finding new ways to get close to me. I need them to go away." The sincerity written on his face showed her he wasn't joking around.

"Get real."

He shook his head. "You don't get it. If I can figure out why you don't like me, I can use that knowledge to get the cologne company off my back. That will also make the women disappear from my life and leave me in peace, so I can concentrate on playing hockey."

"Cologne?"

"They think my sweat turns women on and want to bottle my…smell."

She stared. "That's disgusting."

"You're telling me. Try having your boxers stolen when you slip into the showers after practice or someone trying to lift your luggage at the airport." He stood and paced the room. "I can't stand it anymore."Her phone rang. She walked over and looked at the screen. *Yes!*

Mr. Dogger already needed her. *Goodbye, vacation. Hello, Ferriday house.* "Hang on a second. I need to take this."

She pushed the button. "Hello, Mr. Dogger. How are you?"

He rattled in her ear in short sentences, his voice rising. She grinned and shimmied around the table. "I'll be happy to help you. That'll be double time. I'm on vacation, remember?"

She disconnected the call and squealed. Halfway to the door, she remembered Dominic and paused. "I'm sorry. I need to go back to work. Good luck with your problem."

Dominic hurried over and blocked the door. "I'll pay you five hundred thousand dollars to spend the next two weeks with me at my home, so I can continue to play hockey."

Her head snapped back and she blinked. A half a million dollars?

"You're joking."

"There's nothing funny about my life." He dropped his arms to his sides. "You're my only hope, or I'm going to give up hockey completely and go back to Russia. At least there, I can live in peace. I'm desperate, Diana."

There was no denying he had money, and she knew how much playing hockey meant to him. She bit down on her bottom lip. With that much money, she could quit her job, buy the Ferriday house, and be open for business in no time. Best of all, she'd be debt free and wouldn't have to take out a loan, which would make her parents proud of her.

But she'd have to put up with Dominic for two weeks. She'd end up killing him within three days. She ground her teeth together. It would test all her patience, but she would have more than enough money if she survived staying with him with her sanity intact.

She didn't have to think twice. The Ferriday house was her dream. "I'll do it."

Chapter Two

Dominic's adrenaline kicked into high gear, but he hid his elation over Diana's willingness to help him. Finally, he would have her to himself and she couldn't keep running away and turning him down.

He stood at the top of the employee stairwell, waiting for Diana to come back from kicking the women off the floor of the hotel and informing her boss of her change of plans. He grinned to himself. The first time he caught a glimpse of her at the fundraiser, she'd taken his breath away with her overconfident attitude that made her sexier than hell.

The first time he saw her she'd stuck her nose in the air and turned her back to him when she caught him staring. The result of someone, a woman, snubbing him shocked him into action. He couldn't get her out of his head.

He fumbled over introducing himself, and came right to the point of demanding she go out on a date. It wasn't until Grayson and his friend Juan informed him you don't order a woman to go out to dinner that he'd received his first lesson about the opposite sex.

She started as a challenge to him. A beautiful phenomenon that held the key to his troubles, and gave him hope of changing his life around. The one woman who made him work hard to catch her.

So he politely asked her to go out with him again. Six times. She went from turning him down with an I-don't-think-so to rolling her eyes and walking away without a word. Each time she rejected him, her refusals turned him on more.

Now he was desperate. He wanted her, and he wanted her bad. Since meeting her, his life careened out of control and he realized he needed her. She gave him confidence that he could end his nightmare of attracting woman the way brokers bet on hockey games. Without her showing him what he could do to turn off his charm, he'd kiss his career goodbye and end up living back in Russia.

He loved his homeland, but hockey in America was his life. He lived and breathed time on the ice, competing, and rigid play. The advantages of staying in the United States outweighed going back home and playing in the minor leagues or worse, retiring and becoming a coach.

He wasn't ready to call it quits. The lack of excitement would bore him in a month.

Diana slipped through the doorway, grinning. "All clear. The women are out of the building and walking to the grocery store after I hinted you'd gone out for shaving cream."

He bent over and picked up her purse, handed it to her, and motioned for her to lead the way. "Great. My security team is parked behind the hotel to draw the crowds to the back, while one of the guys parked my car in front of the main entrance. Hopefully, we can make a clean break."

"Smart. They'll never think we're going out in the open. It might buy us more time," she said.

Her soft blond curls bounced with each step. The fire in her hazel colored eyes challenged him. He found himself wanting to tease her, just to have her nail him with that killer look she always threw his way.

He'd tried to stay away and respect her wishes, but during the last couple of months, he found himself thinking about her constantly. She was the most beautiful woman he'd ever seen.

She had him feeling like a beginner in the dating world. When he'd arrived in the United States, he'd quickly learned it was the home of the free. Women asked *him* out. Women paid for *his* dinner. Women slept in *his* bed. Before he knew how it happened, women consumed *his* life.

It was hard for a man to say no, but he'd learned rather fast that saying yes wasn't all it was cracked up to be. Even his friends laughed about his problems. No one took him seriously, but he'd reached his limit. And, now that his coach had given him the ultimatum to lose the women or leave the team, he was desperate. He wanted to be left alone.

Outside the hotel, Dominic nodded at his security team. He placed his hand low on Diana's back and refused to let her shrug him away as he ushered her to the rental car. He planned to head straight to the charter plane and get out of Cottage Grove before news hit the airwaves that he was leaving.

"Wait." Diana braced herself in the doorway of the car and turned around. "I can't go for two weeks with only my purse. I need to pack and find someone to water my plants for me."

He held out his arms. "I'll buy you anything you need."

"Oh no you won't." She smacked him square in the chest with the back of her hand. "Move."

He backed away. Damn. He liked the way she bossed him around and got all in his face.

She marched across the street, holding her hand out in front of her when a car approached. He shook his head in wonder, watching the vehicle slow down and come to a stop. She gave no more attention to the traffic, hopped up on the sidewalk, and disappeared inside a one story blue building.

The sign above the door read Cottage Grove City Hall. He closed the car door, walked around the front fender, and slipped into the driver's spot. Grayson's fiancée and Diana's best friend, Shauna, worked at the City Hall. He'd wait and if she didn't come back out in a few minutes, he'd go get her. The longer he stayed in one place, the bigger chance the women would find him.

He chuckled. The sound in the empty car surprised him. Had it really been that long since he'd heard the sound of his own laughter?

Movement in the rearview mirror caught his eye. He whipped around in the seat and groaned. He'd run out of time.

The women walked four abreast and five deep. He'd rather face two pair of blueliners with only three minutes to go in the game than be at the mercy of the gang of women headed his way.

Thankfully, the shaded windows of the vehicle protected him from the women's view. Unable to go out and help his security team talk sense into the crowd, he waited. Anger grew and he tapped his fist against the steering wheel. This was ridiculous.

He opened the car door. A piercing whistle stopped him from climbing out of the vehicle. Diana removed her fingers from her mouth, motioned for him to shut the door, and marched back across the street toward him.

He closed the door, and watched Diana in fascination. His smile grew broader.

Long, confident steps showed off the length of her legs. He rubbed a hand over his mouth. Her words were lost in the noise of the cluster surrounding the car, but the passion in her expression and the firmness of her chin hinted at the conversation. His body hardened and he sat straighter. Two weeks with Diana would solve all his problems. Every. Single. One.

He hadn't had sex in weeks. Hell, months. Now, suddenly, he wanted Diana Spenner more than he wanted to escape the madness of his life.

The passenger door opened and Diana slipped inside. He stared. Flushed cheeks, bright eyes, and one wayward curl caught in the corner of her mouth left him speechless.

She glanced at him, frowning. "What?"

"Nothing," he said.

"Then drive." She jerked the seatbelt around her and buckled. "Shauna's going to pack a couple of suitcases for me and have them delivered. I need to text her and let her know where we're going."

"Uh." He pulled out onto Main Street. "I rent a condominium during the season."

"Think bigger, Dominic. I need a city…an address."

He'd need blood in his head to think and right now, every ounce of common sense headed south of the border. "Tell her to get the address from Grayson. He's been to my place."

"You don't even know where you live?" Diana snorted. "This is going to be a long two weeks. I hope you don't lose me wherever we go. You seem rather one directional at times, Dominic. I don't understand how you can play hockey. Are you the goalie?"

He growled. "No. I'm not the goalie."

"Well, there's hope." She sighed. "I'm probably going to be bored to death and know way more about hockey than I need to know by the time this job is done. Which none of my gained knowledge will help me on my resume."

He glanced between her and the road. "You're not looking forward to spending time with me…alone?"

"With the amount of money you're paying me, I'll deal with whatever comes my way. I've had worse jobs." She gazed behind her out the back window. "What kind of car are the security guys driving?"

"Black Hummer."

"They're behind us."

"Yes." He pressed his foot down on the accelerator as he left the city limits, trying to keep ahead of the fans and still follow along on the conversation with Diana. "They go everywhere with me."

"Maybe you should quit using them. They only draw more attention to you," she said. "Having the men in black is like holding a neon sign above your head that flashes, 'I'm important, come bother me.'"

"Then who will keep the women away from me?" The thought of being out in public by himself horrified him. The women would rip his clothes off.

"Me. That's what you're paying me for." She pulled out her phone, texted, and then slipped her cell back in her purse.

"Who are you sending a message to?" he asked.

"Not that it's any of your business, but Shauna."

He ran his tongue across his upper teeth. "I'm glad you're staying with me."

"Don't get your hopes up that it's anything more than a job. I need the money." She leaned forward, studied the distance, and then suddenly squealed and stomped her feet on the floor of the car.

"What's wrong?"

She pointed over to the left and ahead of them at a large, old house. "See that beautiful home with the large oak tree in the front yard and the picket fence?"

"Yeah."

"When I'm done working for you, I'm going to buy it." She inhaled and her gaze softened.

He slowed down, studying the large two-story colonial style house. Half the shutters hung crooked. The white paint peeled on the west side, showing its age. Overgrown weeds surrounded a For Sale sign staked in the yard. He couldn't see whatever she saw in the rundown place.

About the only thing it had going for it was location. On the edge of town, it was close enough to take advantage of the quaint community he'd enjoyed while staying here and yet without other houses around, it would provide a quiet atmosphere. He shook his head. A better choice would be to knock the whole thing down and build a nice new home.

"It's not livable. Even the fence is falling down and the upper window is broken." He returned his gaze to the road.

The thought of her staying in a home that could crumble down around her made him uneasy. What was wrong with her staying at the hotel where there were people around and everything was within walking distance?

"It'll be a showpiece when I'm done fixing the house up to its original glory." She rolled her head along the seat rest and smiled. "Did you know it's the oldest house in Cottage Grove? It's practically famous already. It's been vacant for two years and the town wants to sell the lot it sits on. They figure someone will tear the old place down and build a new home or expand the city limits and a huge land developer will build a mini mall or something. Not me. I'd never destroy something as cool as the Ferriday House with all the stories that come with it from age. I'm going to keep the history and make new memories for all the people who will visit the area."

"Why?"

"I want to open a bed and breakfast." She clapped her hands and laughed. "God, that felt good to finally tell someone, even if it's just you. It makes it real. I am going to own a bed and breakfast. There. My secret is out for the next two weeks. Hey, maybe I'll even name the honeymoon suite—" she raised her hands and made air quotes "—Dominic's playroom."

He jerked his gaze off the road to Diana. "What?"

Her brows shot higher and her jaw dropped. "That didn't come out right. Forget I made that suggestion. It just hit me that this is really happening. I can do this, and no one can stop me."

He stared at the road. His hands tightened on the steering wheel. Was that some hidden message? Did she fantasize about him? Maybe she thought he was a playboy.

"Maybe you should think longer about your plans for the future. It's a huge business decision for a woman." He entered the highway and set the cruise control.

"A woman?" She leaned forward and narrowed her gaze. "I've dreamed about that house since I was in high school. When I came back to Cottage Grove after college and started working at the hotel, I knew what I really wanted to do is run my own business. I'm good at my job. My success or failures in life has nothing to do with being a female."

"Whoa." He shook his head. "I didn't say that."

"Sure sounded like it."

"I, um, apologize." He grimaced, hoping the advice he received from the guys on the team about always letting women think they were right would work with Diana. The words sat bitter on his tongue. No woman had forced him to take responsibility for his actions as if he was a six-year-old who'd been caught swiping the cookies.

"Good. Because I'm buying the house and property, and no one is changing my mind." She leaned back.

He relaxed, feeling successful at dodging another argument and continued driving, thinking there was more to Diana than he originally thought. Bossy and independent, she was also determined and goal oriented. He liked that.

"San Jose," he said. Proud of himself for finally remembering the city he called home nine months of the year.

"Huh?"

"That's where I live."

"Oh." She glanced over at him. "I've been there a few times when a group of us drove over on spring break when I went to Berkeley."

"I'll show you around." He glanced at her and winked. "We'll go on a date."

"Nice try, but no." She turned to gaze out the side window.

A genuine smile came over him. Because right before she'd turned away, he'd seen the corners of her mouth twitch. Oh, she'd fight her attraction to him. She'd give him one hell of a challenge. But she wanted him.

Chapter Three

No sooner had Dominic shown her around the gated community where his upscale condominium was located and got her settled in the spare bedroom with the navy colored curtains with matching bedspread and bare walls lacking any homey feel, than he announced it was time for him to go to practice. Diana grabbed her purse off the bed, surprised to find she looked forward to watching a bunch of men beat each other up on the ice.

Men that were not Dominic. What wasn't there to like?

Dominic blocked the doorway of her bedroom. "You can't go wearing that."

She looked down at her clothes. The black slacks, heels, and white blouse the hotel required suited any occasion. "Not much I can do about my clothes until Shauna sends my bags to me. Trust me, I can't embarrass you wearing business attire, and I won't dress like a skank just so you can have bragging rights with the guys on the team."

"Come on." He turned, marched down the hallway, and entered his room.

She stood a step inside the bedroom. The musky aroma she associated with Dominic hung in the air. She swallowed. Goosebumps broke out over her bare arms.

It was true—his scent should be bottled. Every freaking woman in the world would buy the cologne by the truckload. Not that she'd tell him that.

A huge king size bed sat in the middle of the room. Four wooden posts from each corner held white mesh netting and offset the black plush comforter. She studied the area with interest, since it was the first sign that he cared about where he lived and put his own touch to the style of his room. Two framed pictures of winter scenes hung on the wall at the head of his bed. A long, lonely road covered in blown snow and a frozen pond. A black and red rug covered most of the wood floor.

Impressed with his decorating skills, she wondered if one of the women who hung around him all the time helped him pick out the colors. She stepped toward the door Dominic disappeared through.

He walked out of what she guessed to be his closet, holding a sweatshirt, hat, and scarf. He handed the pile to her.

"What's this for?" she asked.

"You'll need it at the rink." He picked up a large duffle bag, almost the length of the bed, with the Sharks logo on the side. "Damn."

"What now?"

He frowned, and the lines between his brows wrinkled. "I forgot to feed you."

"It's okay." She relaxed, deciding that it was rather nice that he was thinking about her comfort.

"No, it's not." He shifted the bag to one hand, reached into his back pocket, and handed her his wallet. "There's money in there. You can buy a coffee to help you stay warm while you watch practice. You can also get some junk food out of the vending machines. Afterward, I'll take you out to dinner and you can have some real food."

Growing up with banker parents who thought it was splurging to grab a dollar burger at McDonald's had taught her the value of money. She warmed, knowing Dominic trusted her with his wallet. His action softened her resolve not to like him.

"I can't use any more of your money." She stuck her hand out, trying to give his wallet back.

"Keep it."

"It won't kill me to wait a few hours. I had a big breakfast." If coffee and a piece of dry toast counted as a hearty meal. She shrugged when he refused to take his wallet back and slipped it on top of her pile of clothes. "Let's hit the court."

"The rink."

"Whatever. I don't even like hockey. I'm more a football fan."

He narrowed his eyes and grumbled about hockey being the only sport worth watching. She pressed her lips together to keep from laughing. Right then, she decided she rather liked the human side of him, the side that showed emotion and got irritated over her teasing.

Dominic was always so serious. He had to laugh more. And, since she'd be spending all her time with him for the next two weeks, it was a problem she could solve while she fought the women away. By the end of the job, she'd break Dominic's tight hold on his self-control and let him experience spontaneity and fun. She'd have him cracking jokes and giving in to late night desires in no time.

She gulped. Maybe not desires. She'd better stick to the jokes.

A fifteen minute drive later, the security team pulled up to the practice arena called the Shark Tank. Tanner, the biggest out of the two men Dominic hired, nodded to his boss before exiting the car. Evan, the other guy who was shorter and more serious, slipped out the door without a word, obviously knowing the routine.

Dominic turned to Diana in the back seat. She hadn't said a word the whole trip, because Tanner eyed her in the rearview mirror the whole way as if speaking would get her handcuffed and thrown out of the car without stopping.

Dominic took the sweatshirt off her lap. "Arms up."

She clasped her hands together. A muscle along his cheek twitched and she tilted her head at the same moment he pulled the sweatshirt over her head. She automatically stuck her arms in the sleeves, peeved that her stubbornness was no match for a guy with fast hands.

As Dominic rolled up the sleeves of the too long sweatshirt, she studied his face. "Do you have a dimple?"

He glanced at her and after a few beats smiled. She gasped. The difference in him stunned her. Oh, he kept the hard edge, but an adorable transformation came over his face making him downright gorgeous and—she gulped again—irresistible.

"Uh, you might not want to smile in public." She inhaled deeply, blew out her cheeks, and let go of the side effects of his smile in one big whoosh.

"I know. It's a lesson I have learned the hard way." He picked the stocking cap up and put it on her head, chuckling.

She rearranged the hat, so it wasn't covering half her face. "What's so funny?"

"Your curls are cute." He flipped the scarf over her head and wrapped it around her neck.

Cute? She kept her hair loose and wild for a reason. Kate had told her men would find the curls sexy. "Thanks a lot," she muttered.

He paused, forcing her to meet his eyes. "I like you wearing my clothes. It's sexy."

His confession caressed her skin and a flutter went through her landing in her lower stomach. Her body warmed, and heat rolled up her spine and settled on her cheeks. His gaze lowered to her mouth, and she moistened her lips.

For seconds, his intense eyes locked onto her, until he finally leaned forward. His mouth hovered inches from her lips. The warmth of his breath brushed her face. She blinked rapidly to keep her eyes open to see what he was going to do next.

The temperature in the car rose. She sucked in air and leaned forward spanning the inches separating them. He was close. Close enough to —

The door opened. She jerked back. Dominic closed his eyes and groaned. She stared in shock. *Oh. My. God.*

Tanner stood outside, but avoided their eyes. "All clear, Dominic."

What was she doing? One more second and she would've kissed him. She tugged at the scarf, struggling to unwind it from her neck. The last thing she needed to do is get physically involved with him.

Dominic laid his hands on top of hers, settling her down. She sagged against the seat. Her insides a quivery mess of sexual lust.

"I know you're hot, but take the scarf. You'll need it when we're inside. It gets cold when you're watching practice," he whispered.

Hot wasn't even close to what she felt. Her blood boiled and every nerve in her body trembled at attention. What was she doing? What was he doing to her? Her weak reaction to him must be his fault. She certainly didn't ask him to kiss her.

She couldn't let herself fall for his charm. Even if he had a dimple that no grown man should be allowed to own and a smile that showed a slight gap between his front teeth, she would not kiss him. She had a job to do, and she wasn't going to allow herself to become one of *those* women who lost total control of their thinking around Dominic.

Outside the vehicle, Dominic walked beside her. There were only a dozen cars parked in the lot. She glanced at the blue sky, thankful for the sweatshirt hanging to her knees. The outfit would come in dead last in a fashion show, but she could use the weather as an excuse for her overheated body.

Twenty feet from the door of the arena, car tires squealed behind them. Tanner wrapped his arms around her, stealing her breath. Dominic sandwiched her from the other side. A group of women screamed their joy inside the car at catching Dominic before practice.

"Idiots," Dominic muttered.

"We'll get rid of them." Tanner let go of Diana.

She found herself thrust into Dominic's embrace. Her sleeves had unrolled during the excitement, and all she could do is stand there with her arms hanging down, pinned to her sides. The clothes situation was going to have to change. If she had to defend herself against other women, she'd do more damage if her arms were usable.

"Let's get you inside." Dominic ushered her up the steps and into the building. "Tanner and Evan will guard the doors for the next two hours. We're safe."

"Your life seriously sucks, dude." She yanked up her sleeves, fixed her scarf, and followed him farther into the building, thankful for the chill in the air.

He stopped at a set of double doors and pointed to their left. "Vending machines are down that way. I need to go change in the locker room. When you're done, go through these doors. You can watch until practice is over."

"Okay." She hiked the sleeve of the sweatshirt and took his wallet out of her purse. "Maybe I'll buy a snack, but I'll pay you back. You can deduct it out of our agreement."

"Diana." He blew out his breath. "We'll discuss this later. I'm going to get suited up. I'll meet you right here after practice."

He lumbered away. She gazed after him, watching his jeans tug against his solid legs. Her stomach growled. Food. That would get her mind off almost kissing him in the car.

Five minutes later, with a coffee in one hand and a Hostess Ding Dong and Dominic's wallet in the other hand, Diana worked her way to the front seats by the rink, right behind the Plexiglas. After fumbling with the flip up seat, she managed to sit down without spilling her drink. The voices from the players echoed in the empty arena. The slice of their skates cut through the air. She shivered, set everything but her coffee in her lap, and cuddled the warm cup between her hands.

Half the players wore red shirts and the other half wore white. Both teams sported the San Jose Sharks logo on their jersey. She studied the men, trying to find Dominic. They all appeared similar in size.

Her gaze landed on number thirty-one. He looked her way, and she waved. She'd recognize his broad shoulders anywhere. He skated toward her, spraying ice when he slid to a stop in front of the see-through protective wall.

He tapped the glass with his hockey stick. "Warm enough?"

She nodded, and twirled her finger in the air. "Turn around."

"Huh?"

"Rotate. I want to see what you wear," she said.

He cocked his head, and pivoted around in a circle. She giggled quietly, liking the way his ass looked in the tight white pants. No wonder women went crazy for him.

Laughter broke out on the rink. She followed Dominic's gaze to the other members of his team and found them pointing at her and slapping each other in amusement. She frowned.

"What's their problem?"

"Probably jealous. Just ignore them." He motioned with his stick. "I need to get back. Two hours and I'll be done."

She stuck her thumb up. "Good luck."

"It's just practice."

"So?" She grinned. "Go kick their ass for laughing at you."

He skated away and by the expression on his face, she knew he was laughing at her. His dimple showed and the skin at the edge of his eyes crinkled. She settled down and opened her Ding Dongs.

Over the course of the next hour, she watched Dominic skate around and pass the puck back and forth. No one seemed to hit the black flat disc toward the goals at the end of the rink, and instead concentrated on playing catch. She shifted and crossed her legs. The wallet on her lap slid, and she caught it before it fell to the sticky floor under her feet. She fingered the black leather.

The five dollars she expected to find earlier when she bought her snacks turned out to be a stack of fifty-dollar bills. Not wanting to snoop, she'd dug through the money and found a twenty folded behind the row of bills to use in the change machine and quickly closed the wallet back up. She slipped her finger in between the folds. Now that she was going to live with Dominic for two weeks, she was curious about what a famous hockey player would carry around with him.

The contents of a wallet said a lot about the owner. She wiggled her finger inside the divider without opening the billfold. Nothing stood out as odd. Maybe if she closed her eyes and used her sense of touch …

She tried again. Her fingernail caught on a paper, or…She opened her eyes. Was that the foil wrapping of a condom?

She jerked her finger out of the wallet, dropping it back on her lap. Her heart raced as if she'd done something illegal. He'd given her the wallet in good faith. She would not snoop. It wasn't any of her business whether he was always prepared for sex.

The team skated off the end of the rink and walked single file to the locker room. She pursed her lips as one by one, she was the only one left in the arena. She wondered if he would use the condom with someone else while she stayed with him.

Her body quivered remembering how close they were to kissing in the car. She swept up her empty cup and wrapper and stood. He'd better not even think about bringing a woman back to the condominium while she was staying with him and having sex.

Chapter Four

Nestled in the back corner of a quiet restaurant in one of the less popular neighborhoods of San Jose, Dominic shrugged off the hood of his sweatshirt. He watched Diana glance around self-consciously in the dim light. She'd insisted they hit the drive-thru window of a fast food restaurant, but he'd wanted to show her a good time. It mattered little to him that she was wearing his clothes.

Getting to know her better was his main objective, and she looked adorable decked out as a Sharks fan. Since almost kissing her in the car, he'd tried to get closer to her after practice and failed. She seemed extra jumpy, and he wanted to make sure she wasn't going to back out of their deal.

"So, how often do you practice?" She fiddled with the edge of her napkin.

He set down his glass of wine. "Twice a week right now, because we have two games per week. The first month it'll all be home games because we're in exhibition season, but next month we're on the road. I have weekends and Thursdays off."

"Your whole life revolves around hockey. I'm surprised you came to help Shauna with the fundraiser." She leaned forward. "Which was cool of you to do, by the way. The changes that are being made around Cottage Grove with the money all the athletes brought in helped a lot."

"Grayson wanted a favor, and I was growing bored." He shrugged. "I enjoy helping. It's hard sometimes…"

"The women?"

"Yes."

"Tell me about this company that's harassing you," she asked.

He ran his hand over his jaw. "Nomora…they produce men's cologne. Their representative is hounding me to provide samples of my sweat, spit, and something about collecting the acidity in my body. They want to provide other men with a way to gain a woman's attention by providing a cologne with the same compounds as the…smell I produce. I've told them, it's not something men will like. They don't believe me."

"No. I don't imagine they would." She snorted quietly and shook her head. "You do know that most men think you're lucky to have the problem you do. Think of all the nice boys who want to be badasses like you. They'd kill to switch spots with you."

"Yeah. I'd gladly trade places with any one of them."

"What happens when you're in Russia?" She lifted her drink. "You said you go there to get away from the chaos."

"That's the thing, nothing happens to me when I go back home." He shook his head. "In the village, everyone knows me. It's a small area. Maybe three thousand people."

"Do you date?" She glanced away. "I mean, when you're home."

"No."

"Huh." She sipped her wine.

He braced his forearms on the table. "Why did you do that?"

"Just hard to believe. I would think you had a girlfriend back home, since you don't seem to have one here in the States. At least when I Google you, the articles pin you as a playboy, not a relationship sorta guy," she said.

The waitress brought their food. He leaned back, catching the wink the woman gave him. He ignored her.

"My name's Kimmy. If you'd like anything else…I mean anything, just ask for me." She slipped a piece of paper under the lip of his plate.

Disgust soured his mood. He slid the folded message back to the edge of the table. "I'm not—"

"He's mine." Diana laid her hand atop his, and smiled at him without looking at the waitress. "Aren't you, baby?"

"I, uh, yeah, all yours." He curled his fingers around her hand, catching on to her act. "Sweetcheeks."

The waitress stared at the two of them. He continued to gaze at Diana. She was full of surprises.

"Enjoy your dinner." The waitress spun around and hurried away.

Diana jerked her hand back. "Sweetcheeks? Really? You might as well have said, 'Hey, chubs, want another piece of cake?'"

"I'd never say such a thing." He glanced down at the table before looking at Diana again. "What should I call you?"

"Diana." She popped a fry into her mouth and grinned. "Seriously, Dom. Did you see the woman's face? I thought she was going to cry. I think we're onto something with this whole fake dating thing."

"I told you. I need you." He grinned, feeling proud of getting her to come stay with him.

"Stop right there." She shook her head. "No smiling. At least until we're back at your condominium. You don't want to press your luck and have Kimmy coming back to our table."

"You're right." He tapped the edge of the table. "Scoot over here to my side."

"Why?"

"Maybe if we looked like a real couple, we'll get through the whole meal without any more interruptions." He scooted to the inside of the booth.

"Good idea." She pushed her plate over, hiked up her sweatshirt, and slid into the spot next to him.

Her leg pressed against the side of his thigh. His body went on instant alert. He reached for his wine and accidently bumped his elbow into her arm. "Sorry."

"No problem." She had plenty of room to scoot over, but she remained next to him.

He leaned over and whispered, "Kiss me."

She burst out laughing. "We're pretending. Don't confuse reality with fantasy."

"I won't…my little lamb."

She flattened her hands on the table, turned her head, and nailed him with a look that made it hard not to laugh. "No. Just. No."

He leaned forward, propped his hand over his lower jaw, and hid his smile. Hell, he was going to have a good time with her. She gave him back everything he dished out without turning it into a game to get his attention.

They spent the rest of the meal in comfortable conversation. The longer he went without any interruptions, the more relaxed he started to feel. When he finished all the food on his plate and ate most of the dessert Diana wanted to share, he leaned back and stretched. This was the most enjoyable meal he'd eaten since leaving Russia.

Diana yawned. A smile landed on his lips. Her guard had slipped during the meal, and she hadn't even noticed they'd conversed without any of her normal snappy replies.

"It's been a long day with traveling and springing everything on you. Let's get you home." He gently nudged her, moving her to her feet.

What he really wanted to do was wrap his arm around her, let her lean her head against him, and take her straight to his bedroom. Without her defenses up, she came across soft and warm, much more accepting of being in his company. He quickly paid their tab, phoned the security team, and met them in front of the restaurant doors with the Hummer ready to go.

Diana slid across the back seat and leaned her head against the window. He sat and stretched out his legs. Now that they were making progress and getting along, he was glad for the weekend ahead. All he wanted to do was hide out at the house, and see how many more chips he could make in her armor.

He laid his arm along the back of the seat. His hand touched the curls popping out from the back of her stocking cap. He grinned in the darkness of the car. She'd forgotten all about wearing the hat while in the restaurant. It'd almost be a disappointment when her luggage arrived. He'd like to keep her wearing his clothes.

He closed his eyes. A feisty Diana wearing one of his jerseys with nothing else came to mind. Her bare legs peeking out from under the material as she curled up at the end of his couch gave him something to look forward to in the next couple of days. He'd finally be able to find out if she painted her toes to match the soft pink color on her fingernails.

A weight pressed against his leg. He pried one eye open and peeked. Diana had lain down across the seat. The top of her head rested against his thigh. He lifted his hand, but caught himself before caressing her head. She needed her sleep. He'd thrown a lot at her today.

No sooner had he got used to feeling her beside him than Tanner drove into the garage. Dominic looked down at Diana, hating to wake her.

"Will you need us over the weekend?" Tanner asked.

"No. I'll call if we do."

"Very good, sir." Tanner hesitated. "Earlier we received a call of a delivery, and I had one of our guys take it into your house."

He nodded. "Thanks."

The doors closing never fazed Diana. She only squirmed against him and curled her legs tighter to her chest. He tapped her shoulder and waited.

Nothing. She continued sleeping without a care in the world.

Feeling as if he was taking his life in his hands, he opened the side door and did what any other man would do. He picked her up and cradled her in his arms. She sighed and snuggled her head underneath his chin.

Sue him for taking the time to dip his head and inhale the sweet feminine scent that'd teased him all day. He shifted her closer and carried her through the garage.

At the door into the house, he fumbled with the knob, but succeeded in getting them both inside. He strode through the kitchen, down the hallway, and into her bedroom. Without turning on the light, he walked to the bed.

His toe caught on something heavy. When he went to right himself, he stepped on something large. His upper body careened forward, while his feet scrambled for solid ground and met air. Refusing to let Diana go down with him, he heaved her toward the bed before falling on the floor.

Her scream pierced his ears and cut off instantly when she bounced on the mattress. He struggled to his knees, cussing under his breath. It took him time to climb out of the maze of items littering the floor, but he eventually reached the wall where he flipped the light on.

Six suitcases in varying sizes lay scattered in front of the bed. His gaze traveled to Diana, and seeing her safe and unhurt, he laughed.

Sprawled on the bed, her hat knocked lopsided with her curls jumping in all different directions was a sight to see. But it was the indignant pose of a princess getting knocked off her pedestal that tickled him.

"You threw me." She reached to pull off her hat, but the sleeves of the sweatshirt had unrolled making the task impossible.

"I tripped." He bent over laughing, bracing his hands on his knees.

She huffed and scooted off the bed. "Honestly, the women that go ape shit over you should live with you. Twelve hours of constant Dominic would show them the error of their thinking."

"It was either drop you or throw you." He straightened. "You're lucky I was able to toss you as far as the bed."

Her mouth formed a circle and she fisted her hands on her hips, the ends of the sweatshirt dangling down the sides of her legs. "Jeez, what is it with you always calling me fat?"

He snuffed his amusement, rubbing his hands over his face. "I'm not."

"Sounded like it."

"You're perfect. I'll leave you alone to go through your luggage." He turned around, and because he loved seeing her temper, he couldn't pass along another message. "Sweet dreams… sweetcheeks."

He cleared the doorway as one of the small suitcases smashed into the wall across the hallway from her room. He laughed until his stomach hurt. A door slammed as he walked into his bedroom. He headed straight to the bathroom. A pleasurable ache of lust settled over him. A cold shower was the last thing he wanted when there was a warm sexy woman staying down the hallway.

Chapter Five

Used to waking at five in the morning to go to work, Diana rose early and made her way out of the bedroom after her shower. She glanced at Dominic's door and found it closed. The house was quiet, so she headed to the kitchen. Every cell in her body hoped athletes were allowed to drink coffee and she'd find some in his cupboards.

She sagged in relief to find an assortment of different coffees plus sweeteners above the coffee maker in the cabinet. After getting everything set up, all she had to do was wait for the first cup to start her morning.

With an empty cup cradled in both hands, she sat at the table gaining her bearings while the coffee maker ran. Yesterday's events rushed to the forefront. What was she doing?

She'd skipped town with Dominic with no word to her folks, or a way for Mr. Dogger to get ahold of her. She dropped her chin and frowned at the mug. Women her age went on vacation all the time, and she'd gone away to college for four years and lived independently from her parents. She was twenty-four years old, more than old enough to go off with a man alone and enjoy herself.

Not that working for Dominic was a pleasure vacation. It was a game with a prize at the end. A very big prize that'd change her life.

Except, she couldn't figure out who was playing who. A half a million dollars for hanging around Dominic was a joke. Either Dominic was plain stupid or she had lost her mind. Taking his money for doing practically nothing…well, it almost made her a whore.

Not that she was going to sleep with him.

She dug her cell out of the back pocket of her jeans, and hit the button for her parents' house. The answering machine clicked on, and she left a brief message letting them know she'd be back in two weeks. No reason to upset them or discuss what she was doing, she kept her explanation short with enough details in case she became involved in a car accident and lost her memory. No one needed to know she'd pimped herself to a big, badass Russian named Dominic.

She inhaled deeply. He was a hot mess.

The few times yesterday when he'd appeared almost normal, she'd found herself excited to spend time with him. Okay, "excited" was too enthusiastic of a way to describe the flutters in her belly and the urge to learn more about him. Maybe "unburdened by the job she'd agreed on performing" fit the occasion better. She could even admit to enjoying their dinner together, and watching a team of buff hockey players glide around in front of her turned out to be more interesting than it'd originally sounded.

The coffee maker quieted. She stood and filled her cup before moving over to the fridge, sniffing the milk to make sure it was still good, and adding a few drops to her coffee.

"Morning." Dominic's rough voice came from behind her.

She swallowed too fast, burnt her tongue, and whirled around. "Good mor—"

Male, hard, muscled body filled the entrance to the kitchen. Boxers hung low on his hips. Blond hair mussed and a night's worth of whiskers roughened the otherwise flawless face—except for the light white scar near his brow that only added to his sexiness. She stepped around the table. Unable to take her gaze off the naked expanse of his body, but knowing she had to put distance between his body and hers, she bumped into the counter in her retreat.

"You're an early riser. I thought I'd beat you out of bed and have coffee made." He strode across the kitchen. "Did you sleep well?"

She nodded, and realizing he wasn't looking at her said, "Yeah." The muscles along his back bulged, twitched, and otherwise hypnotized her. She stared. He reached up for a mug, and her eyes were drawn to the back of his shorts, straining against his ass.

She could die happy. Never had she seen a man with enough muscle in his derriere. She swallowed another sip, grimacing as the liquid flowed over the tip of her tongue stinging the spot she'd burnt.

"I'll call for breakfast. What do you feel like eating?" He glanced over his shoulder at her.

She jerked her gaze away. "Don't you have bread?"

"No."

"Cereal?"

He shook his head. "I don't cook."

"You order all your meals?" She set the cup on the table. "That's a waste of money and unhealthy. I can't believe a professional athlete could live on food loaded with preservatives and cooked in fat."

He slapped his hand on his chest and scratched his pectoral muscle. "I have to eat to survive. It's a necessity."

"Well, we're not eating out every meal while I'm here. You might be able to handle the extra calories, but I'll bloat up like a balloon. I'll cook." She stood, needing to escape. "I'll go grocery shopping."

"Now?"

"Yeah. Why not?" she said.

"I'm not dressed."

"You really shouldn't be traipsing around in your boxers either, but that has nothing to do with me going shopping alone." She forced herself to look him in the eyes.

"It's my house." He leaned his hip on the counter and crossed his arms, making his muscles pop. "Maybe you should evaluate why seeing me in my boxers seems to make you...uncomfortable."

"It doesn't."

"Are you sure?" His chest rose and fell. "Your cheeks are flushed and you seem to have difficulty breathing deeply."

She pushed out a laugh. "It's called underwear for a reason. You don't see me standing here in my bra and panties."

His gaze dropped and he tilted his head. "I don't believe you're wearing panties."

"I am!" She crossed her ankles. "A thong. Not that it's any business of yours."

The corner of his mouth lifted. "What color?"

"Shuttup."

"It's black, isn't it?"

"Red." She shot him a glare. "That was unfair."

He closed his eyes and sighed. "I may now stop breathing."

"While you die, I'm going to buy some food with your money. What a deal." She walked past him and set her cup in the sink.

"The closest market is two miles away. Take my car." He opened a drawer, removed a set of keys, and handed them to her.

She hesitated. "I can't drive the Hummer. It's too big."

"These are to my other car. It won't be too big, trust me." He grinned.

Five minutes later, she slipped the black Porsche out of the garage. Alone, she laughed as she slipped the gear into third and sailed through the gated community in the early morning hour. If she had a top of the line piece of car candy, she wouldn't rely on a security team to drive her around. She'd be speeding around the back streets with the windows down and the radio cranked, showing her sexy and loving every minute of it.

In the parking lot of the store, two men stopped and stared after her. She waved. Oh yeah, she could get used to this. A Porsche beat her old dependable Chevrolet she'd driven since she got her license at sixteen years old and bought for five hundred dollars. The old beater saw her through college and a few fender benders, and still worked perfectly fine.

She flounced into the store with Dominic's wallet in hand, filling the shopping cart with everything she'd need for a week. On a whim, she grabbed a container of vanilla ice cream and four Butterfingers before calling it quits.

When she arrived back at the condominium, she took an extra circle around the block before pulling into the garage and shutting off the engine. Dominic came out and helped her carry the groceries into the kitchen.

Dressed in a black T-shirt and faded pair of Levis that hugged his ass, he stepped into the garage. She followed him inside, making sure she looked him over while his back was to her because if he caught her sneaking a glimpse, he'd turn it into something sexual. It wasn't. She was simply learning more about the man she was going to live with for the next two weeks.

"Is there any kind of food you can't stand?" She left the eggs out on the counter. "Speak now, or be poisoned later."

He seemed to read the side of a box of cereal. "No. I guess not."

She glanced at him again. "Is something wrong with the cereal?"

"Did you know they put riddles on the back of the box?" he said.

"Welcome to my world, Dom." She opened cabinets until she found a skillet. "We're in luck. You have kitchen supplies."

"The condo came furnished when I bought it. If you need something, let me know. I'll have Tanner go out and buy whatever it is and bring it to the house," he said.

"That's okay. If I need something I'll go get it." She cracked eggs into a bowl.

He approached the stove, watching her. "You like my car."

It wasn't a question. She'd be an idiot if she said no. "Yes."

"I'll let you drive for the entire time you're with me if you go out on a date with me."

"Sure." She grinned. "Be prepared to find your own way home though."

"You'd dump me for my car?" He feigned shock.

She laughed. "In a heartbeat. Now, get out of here and let me finish our breakfast."

"Only because I'm starving, I'll go." He grabbed the keys to the Porsche off the counter and pocketed them, eyeing her suspiciously. "Just in case you get any wild ideas. I'll keep these with me now that I know how you really feel about my car."

"Chicken," she called after him, laughing.

A half hour later, she had two plates of omelet and buttered toast on the table when the doorbell rang. She hurried into the living room.

"Go eat. I'll go see who came over." She motioned to the door. "Are you expecting anyone?"

"Gary." Dominic stood and tossed the newspaper on the couch.

She smiled, excitement filling her. "Gary Satchel?"

"Yes…" He hesitated. "Don't tell me you like Gary, and not me."

"I love Gary." She turned and hurried to the front door.

Maybe she exaggerated her feelings to play with Dominic's ego, but after meeting Gary in Cottage Grove two months ago, she'd found the professional football player easygoing and a good sport. They'd played darts at the Quayside Lounge late into the night over a few drinks, and she'd found out they had a lot in common, besides their friendship with Shauna and Grayson Schyler. Lucky for her, she and Gary enjoyed each other's company but there wasn't a spark between them to be found.

She opened the door.

Gary rushed her. She barely had time to prepare herself for one of his bear hugs when Dominic dove in front of her, plowing into Gary. Both men fell against the wall.

"Watch your hands," Dominic growled, pushing Gary as he stepped away. "She's a lady. You'll hurt her if you hug like you tackle out on the field."

"Tackle?" Gary laughed. "It's called a hug, man. Try it sometime, spread the love."

"We don't need any love spreading going on around here either. Just back off and keep your hands to yourself," Dominic muttered.

Gary raised his brows and glanced between her and Dominic. "Ah…so that's how it is, huh?"

"That is *not* how it is." She shot Dominic a scowl, and slapped his arm with the back of her hand before moving over to Gary and slipping her arm around his elbow. "Ignore him. He's cranky and needs to eat. You can come in and join us for breakfast. Tell me what you're doing here. Have you talked to Shauna and Grayson?"

"I came to see you, sexy." Gary threw his arm around her shoulders and hugged her to his side.

"Bullshit," Dominic mumbled behind them.

Gary laughed. "What's with the big Russian?"

Good question. Dominic's mood shifted drastically after Gary arrived. She glanced over her shoulder and caught Dominic's eye. His gaze heated and his lips thinned. He had no reason to be upset with her.

She forced herself to turn around and go dish up the extra omelet she'd made in case Dominic wanted an extra helping. She returned to the table and instead of sitting down in the closest chair next to Gary, she sat at the end between the two men.

The heat of Dominic's gaze warmed her cheeks. She glanced over at him, ready to cut him down with a sarcastic remark if he said anything about her choice of where she sat. Instead, he picked up his fork and started eating.

The moan of appreciation over his first bite of her cooking left her happy. One thing she knew how to do well was cook from scratch. She couldn't wait to feed the visitors to her bed and breakfast after she purchased the Ferriday House.

Chapter Six

Dominic was going to kick Gary's ass. Then he'd ban him from ever coming over to the condominium again. When Gary had called and asked if he could stay for a few hours during a layover on his way to Florida, Dominic had forgotten that Diana and his best friend had formed a friendship back in Cottage Grove during the fundraiser.

Hell, they might as well get a room for how much they were touching each other. He glared at Gary. Why did he have to put his hand on her arm every time he opened his mouth?

"That was the best breakfast I've had in a long time, Diana. Thank you." Gary pushed his empty plate forward and leaned back in his chair, an expression of satisfaction all over his face.

"You're welcome." She stood and took all three of their dishes into the kitchen.

Dominic waited until she ran the faucet, and then leaned over the table. "You have to leave."

"I've still got—he glanced at his watch—an hour and forty minutes before I have to head back to the airport."

"Buy a drink in the lounge and wait like a normal person," he said.

Gary laughed, and then lowered his voice. "Wait? I thought this was a business deal you worked out with Diana. Are you telling me she's here because you two have hooked up?"

"Keep it down," he said. "Not yet, but you're making me look like shit."

Gary latched his fingers behind his head and flexed his biceps. "I do that without trying, bro."

Dominic spotted Diana coming back to the table and shut his mouth. She hugged Gary and told him goodbye.

"You're not going to keep me company?" Gary stood.

She shook her head. "We got in late last night and I need to go put away my clothes before Dom fires me for messing up one of his bedrooms. I'll leave you two to talk."

"When you go back home, tell Shauna she better be taking care of my man Grayson." Gary winked.

"Is there any doubt she loves him to an unhealthy obsession?" She laughed before walking out of the room.

Right now, Dominic wished some of Shauna's deep belief in Grayson rubbed off on Diana. He could use the help to convince her to give him a chance.

"Listen, man." Gary planted his hands on the table and leaned over. "You've gotta romance her. You're all stiff and serious. Women need pretty words—"

"I tried that. She thinks I called her fat."

Gary's brows rose. "Jesus…I don't see how you've stayed alive this long."

"What do I do?"

"Find something you both enjoy. Keep her mind on something else, besides you." He lowered his voice. "I remember watching her dance with her friends back in Cottage Grove. She's seriously hot, bro. Take her dancing."

"I suck at dancing."

"Have her teach you. You're so used to women throwing themselves at you, not even lifting a finger, you've got to step it up. Diana isn't one of your admirers, but she is a woman…a damn hot one. Treat her special." Gary straightened. "Now, I'm gonna take your advice and get out of here. Give you two some space. Nipple up, man. Don't disappoint the male race."

He saw Gary out, and returned to the living room. If he asked her to go out clubbing, she'd tell him no. He flopped down on the couch. What he needed to do was find a way she'd agree to go out with him that'd leave her with no excuse to turn him down.

Taking her out in public meant he'd put himself in harm's way of the women without his security team. He ran his hands over his face in frustration. It wasn't the first time he wished he could lead a normal life.

Diana walked into the room. "Hey. Did Gary leave?"

"Yeah." He put his feet on the floor and sat straighter.

"Oh." She sat across from him in the chair. "It was nice to see him again. It's weird, but I was just thinking that if Shauna hadn't moved back to Cottage Grove to go after Grayson, I never would've met Gary…or you. It's weird how things work out, don't you think?"

"I guess." He studied her, but when she shrugged and crossed her legs without another word, he let her fascination with his friend go. "I think we need to expose our relationship."

"Our relationship?"

"Yes, it's all about you pretending to be my girlfriend." He nodded. "Because I play for the Sharks, everywhere I go they usually write a column in the paper about where I went, who I was seen with, and then they predict if I've become attached."

"Gossip," she murmured.

"Yes."

"You want me to do more than go to your practices?"

"I think we should go out on a date." He held up his hand when she opened her mouth. "A pretend date. That way Nomora and the women will see what I'm doing in my private life."

She sighed. "If we must."

"We do." He stood and crossed his arms across his chest. He liked the new dominating orders he was giving her. "I think we should go to a nightclub, have a few drinks, and maybe dance during a couple of songs. We'll let people take pictures of us together. We'll do that tonight. Tomorrow, we'll go out somewhere else. Maybe to dinner. Being seen with you two nights in a row will have people speculating on our relationship."

"Bed shopping." She pursed her lips.

He grinned, practically patting himself on the back. This was working out better than he'd hoped. He had her thinking about beds, which meant sex with her was still in his future.

"I already have a bed. A very good one," he said.

"No. We need to be seen together bed shopping. A real girlfriend wouldn't want to sleep with you where you've had sex a million times," she said.

He scoffed and when she arched her perfectly manicured brows, he realized she truly believed he slept with all the women who threw themselves at him. No wonder she thought so little of him. Any denying on his part would make him look guilty, and he was guilty, not that he'd confess to her.

"Great idea." He picked his cell off the end table. "I'll make reservations at a club I know of downtown. We'll get the VIP room. They all love me there."

"Make sure the thugs you hire as bodyguards don't come. We have to be alone."

"Okay." He walked over to the window, turning his back on her.

It took him no time to arrange their night. When he was done, he smiled. Date planning was easier than he thought.

"Do I have time to go shopping? Shauna only packed one dress for me." She wrinkled her nose. "It's...well, I've never worn it."

"It'll be fine."

"I could take the Porsche. It wouldn't take much time at all. I'd be in and out." She stood. "I have my own money, so you don't have to worry about me owing you."

He shook his head. "There's no reason to buy a new dress for a night at a club. You'll be fine with whatever you decide to wear."

"What's that supposed to mean?"

It wasn't so much her posture or her words. Her tone announced he'd said something wrong. He played the conversation back in his mind. Diana was out of his league. Women fell for his words, his attention, but she looked for anything to dig her claws into.

"You're beautiful." He spoke softly and slowly. "I would enjoy taking you out in public wearing my jersey and nothing else."

She blinked at him without saying a word. A smile curled the edges of his lips in satisfaction. He'd stunned her speechless.

The gush of disgust came seconds later. "Ugh. You are such a perv."

He held his hands out to the sides of him. "What did I say now?"

She clamped her lips together, pivoted, and marched down the hallway with her hips swaying. He leaned to follow the side-to-side action, and flinched when she slammed the bedroom door.

What the hell? She's mad because I was being honest?

Chapter Seven.

"I'm going to kill Shauna." Diana slammed the last dresser drawer shut.

Not only had her best friend packed the one dress Diana wasn't brave enough to wear, but Shauna also knew she'd bought it on a dare when Kate announced wearing a sexy dress was the only way to get a man. She gazed down at her chest. Talk about major spillage.

Away from home, she had nothing to wear as a cover and donning her winter ski jacket would make her a laughing joke if her picture ended up in the newspaper. She raised her arms, testing the dress, and sure enough, her boobs popped over the top of the material.

Two knocks on the door sent her shimmying to pull the dress back into position.

"It's time to go." Dominic's voice broke through her panic.

She slowly walked to the bed, pressing her arms against her ribs, and slipped into her heels. If she barely moved, she might make it through the evening without flashing everyone at the club. "Hang on."

Not ready to show the world parts of herself that rarely saw daylight, she cracked the door open. "You wouldn't happen to have any ladies' clothes in your room leftover from one of your skanky friends, would you?"

Dominic shook his head. "No."

"Oh." She peered through the opening. "I might have a little problem then…"

"What can I do?"

"I'm not sure."

"Let's start with you telling me what the problem is," he said.

"Promise you won't laugh?" She waited for him to agree, and then shut the door.

Double-checking her dress, she turned the handle and walked out into the hall. She sucked in her bottom lip and clamped her teeth.

Dominic's gaze raked over her with unbridled lust. She turned around, warmth filling her chest. The dress had to go.

"I'll wear the slacks and blouse I wear to work." She managed to take one step before Dominic grasped her hand.

"Don't." He spoke softly. "You're perfect. More than perfect, you're stunning."

She turned. "Really?"

"Absolutely." He held her hand in the air and twirled her.

She clasped her hand to her chest, keeping her dress in place. "Dancing might be tricky."

His eyes gleamed. "I'd have to disagree."

"Dom." Her tone warned him to step back.

He crooked his finger and motioned for her to follow. "I can solve the problem."

In the living room, he held his black blazer open in front of him. She walked to him, sliding her arms into the sleeves. The jacket fell to mid-thigh, past her dress and big enough to wrap around her twice.

He rolled the sleeves above her elbows. She posed, feeling more like a football player with the added padding on her shoulders.

"Mm…" Dominic stepped back and appraised her new outfit.

"Too much? Too manly? Too stupid to be seen at the club when every other woman will be knock out gorgeous?"

"Hell no," he whispered. "Even better. No one can argue with us about our relationship. You're my woman."

What was it with him enjoying seeing his clothes on her? She pulled her hair out from under the collar, choosing to ignore his kink for tonight, because she sorta dug the *I'm taken* style that came with wearing his jacket.

He hesitated before opening the door. She ran into his back, clutched his shirt, and steadied herself. The four-inch heels were higher than she normally wore.

"Are you sure we shouldn't call the security team?" he asked. "It'd be safer."

"We need to look authentic. Nobody will believe we're lovers out for a night of alone time if we're dragging your thugs around."

"Stay close to me." He sighed. "I don't want you getting hurt."

To her delight, he handed the keys to the Porsche over to her. She grinned as she slid into the driver's seat. The leather seats caressed the back of her legs.

A few times during the drive, she sped over the speed limit. She glanced at Dominic. He smiled as if he understood her desire to ignore the rules for the night. She tried to pretend the excitement racing through her veins came from operating the Porsche.

Driving was only the whip cream on her piece of Dominic pie. Alone, he gave her all of his attention. The spark of attraction hovered below the surface, becoming harder to ignore. It was in the way he helped her into his jacket, the way his gaze heated her core, and the way it felt to sit beside a man almost twice her size and come away feeling feminine and cared for.

For once, she enjoyed forgetting about her personal deadline she'd set to own a bed and breakfast, or her job at the hotel, or how her parents would freak when she splurged out on her own and gambled with her life savings by buying the Ferriday House. Tonight was all about her and Dom, even if they were only pretending.

Somehow when they arrived at their destination, Dominic arranged a way through the backdoor of the Pulse nightclub.

Rushed through the stairway and sequestered into the VIP room on the second floor overlooking the dance floor and bar, she collapsed in a chair, laughing.

"The point of being seen in public was to actually mingle with the crowd." She wiggled out of his jacket, hitched her dress higher, and peered out to the packed club below them. "This is wild. I'm definitely no longer at the Quayside, but I'm afraid no one will see us up here all alone."

"I'm not so sure we should do this." He sank down onto the chair. "I don't want you getting mixed up in the crowd."

"Oh, come on, Dom." She leaned forward. "Live a little."

The waitress came in their room. Diana glanced down, making sure her dress stayed put. When she peered back at the woman, it wouldn't have mattered if she was naked and doing the hula hoop. Dominic had the woman's whole attention.

This time, she wasn't giving an inch. She reached over and slipped her fingers into his hand. He gave her a squeeze back.

"What would you like to drink?" he asked.

"Depends. Are you driving or am I?"

He chuckled. "I will."

"Blue Lagoon then."

Dominic shifted to the waitress. "My girlfriend will have a Blue Lagoon. I'll have whatever beer you have on tap."

The waitress sighed. "I get off in an hour. Will you still be here?"

Dominic's mouth opened, and before he could say anything, Diana stood and separated the woman from her pretend boyfriend. "Let's get something straight. That's my man. Hands off, or things will get ugly real fast, chica. Got it? Oh, and before you leave, you might want to spread the news to everyone. I'm in a bad mood tonight, and it isn't going to take much for me to go crazy on someone interrupting my night."

The woman frowned. "I'll be back."

"I'll be ready." She hitched up her dress, and remained standing while the woman left.

When it was safe to let down her guard, she returned to the table. Dominic stared. She shrugged self-consciously.

"Don't get any wild ideas that my rushing to your defense meant anything." She glanced at him below her lashes. "This is all an act. I kind of got caught up in playing the badass."

"That was the hottest thing I've ever seen," he whispered.

She laughed, relaxing. Hot or not, it was fun to pretend she was tougher than she normally was.

To be on the safe side, she slipped his jacket back on. Then she double checked her dress and exhaled in relief when she stayed covered. If she had to use her muscles to get rid of the waitress when she returned, she'd be ready.

The song changed below them. She turned and leaned over the railing. The atmosphere infectious, she danced in her seat enjoying the music.

"Do you want to dance?"

She shook her head. "Not yet, unless you want to go down there with everyone."

"I'm good." He pointed. "See the guy in the black shirt next to the blonde with the dark blue dress?"

Next to the bar, she spotted the couple. He had his arm around the woman and she hung on to him as if she'd had too many drinks. "I see them."

"That's Craig Fresnick. Our goalie." Dominic scooted his chair closer to the railing.

"His girlfriend's pretty."

He chuckled. "It's not his girlfriend."

"Oh."

Growing up in Cottage Grove with Grayson, and him being a former Wimbledon champion, she should've known that. He'd paraded models and movie stars around everywhere before Shauna came back to town. She glanced at Dominic. He watched the couple with an unreadable expression.

Why did it bother her to think in two weeks when she went back to real life, Dominic would be down there with his arm around any female he wanted? He had his pick of choices, any one of them more beautiful than the next.

Movement caught her eye and she turned. At least a dozen women followed the waitress into their private room. They surrounded Dominic before she could prepare for what was guaranteed to come.

"Hey, back off." She stood, glad for the jacket making her look bigger.

They ignored her. Dominic closed his eyes briefly and held his hands in front of him. She pushed her way around the table and grabbed arms, yanking the women away. Stickier than rubber glue, they only wiggled their way back between her and Dominic.

They were outnumbered. She planted her hands on her hips, staring between the bodies at Dominic, who now stood pressed against the railing. This was crazy. She had to do something.

She stuck two fingers in her mouth and blew. Her whistle would deafen anyone in a five-foot radius. Every head turned her way. Using a woman's shoulder for balance, she stepped up onto Dominic's vacant chair.

"Back. Off. Now." She glared at the crowd, while pointing at Dominic. "He's mine."

The women glanced between her and back to their eye candy. She whistled again, grabbing their attention. "Out, before I pull those pretty hair extensions and get you all thrown out of here. Trust me, girls. You do not want me to go there."

Slowly, the women shuffled away from Dom and headed toward the door. Dominic lifted their drinks out of the server's hands before she made her exit and set them on the table. Diana leaned over and gave him a high five.

The last woman, a tall one even without her heels, reached over, plucked Dominic's hair, and seemed to study the few strands pinched between her fingers. Diana hopped down and scooped the hair out of her hand. "I don't think so, bitch."

"I'm from Nomora. I'd like a few—"

"Absolutely not." She stalked the women out of the room, shut the door, and locked her and Dominic inside. Brushing her hands off, she returned to her pretend date. He handed her glass to her.

"To the best girlfriend I've ever had." He held up his beer.

She clinked her glass against his. The lust in Dominic's gaze told her the date was going a little too well. She'd have to bring him back down to earth. "Lucky for you, she's well worth the money."

Chapter Eight

"I think you should get a restraining order against Nomora. Stealing your hair is a crime, or should be." In the last hour, Diana had moved her chair closer to his. "The more I think about it, the company is getting desperate. Sending a woman in to do their dirty work, getting physical and expecting you to be okay with it because you're a male, well that's disgusting."

"The police department will only laugh at me. I've contacted them before, more than once, to have them escort the women away from the arena and my condominium," he said. "Although, I've never had one pull my hair to get a sample without asking first."

To Dominic's surprise, the night passed in continual play back and forth between him and Diana. The music shifted to slower songs, and the noise dimmed the later the hour grew. They'd achieved nothing they'd come to the club for, but he'd gained so much more.

The spirit inside Diana caught him unaware. Her positive outlook on life, including her love of her friends, family, and town had him missing Russia in a good way. He counted his blessings rather than dwell on the difficulties he faced in the United States.

"Do you want another drink?" He'd waited upstairs while she'd retrieved them both another order from the bar earlier, but she seemed in no hurry to grab more.

"Two is a good limit."

He grinned. "I'm still driving home."

She patted his hand. "Please?"

"Next time." He caught her fingers and pulled her closer.

They both leaned toward each other. He stroked the back of her hand with this thumb. Dainty and smooth, she seemed fragile but he knew differently after seeing her in action defending him against the other women.

"Thanks for coming with me tonight." He spread her fingers, linking his hand with hers.

"I've had fun," she whispered. "More than I imagined I would."

He lifted his gaze. "Me too."

All during his career playing hockey, he'd experienced many highs. Goals made, penalty shots that'd won the game, but her confession went right to his soul. He never wanted the night to end. His voice grew husky. "Dance with me."

"Down there?" She glanced over the railing. "I'm not sure that's a good idea after what happened."

He shook his head. "Here. Just you and me."

"Okay."

As if they had all the time in the world, they slowly stood, hands still linked together, and moved to the center of the room. So intent on watching her, he simply stood in front of her. Whether it was from the dim light behind her or the prospect of them going to hold each other, her blue eyes darkened.

She wet her lips with her tongue, staring into his eyes. The move snapped him into action, and he pulled her toward him, wrapping his arm around the back of her waist, while holding her other hand to his chest. Her smoldering gaze slid to his, and a fierce need to protect her came over him.

Unaccustomed to dancing, he took his cue from Diana and swayed to the music. She laid her head against his chest. His breath quickened in response, and her body relaxed against his. Together they fell into a rhythm.

The music changed, but neither one of them seemed to be ready to stop. He closed his eyes, confident that his feet could continue moving without him watching.

Stomach to chest, thigh to leg, pressed together tighter than a perfectly fit puzzle piece, he simply held her. Inhaling the sweet scent of jasmine from her curls, he let go of worrying about how he was doing on their date. He forgot about their agreement, and even that she was only pretending to be his girlfriend. Never had he had the chance to enjoy a woman on his terms, in his own time.

Best of all, he wasn't alone. He was so damn tired of being alone.

With Diana, there was no rush, no pawing, and no desire to explain why they were dancing. He could enjoy their time together and experience all the emotions that came with something new. Already highly addicted to what he had with Diana, he knew no other woman in his life had every brought him this much contentment to enjoy the situation.

Being comfortable with her, and losing time they shared together beat the hell out of the fast pace of fighting women off and taking a one-night stand when he gave up on fighting.

He lowered his hand on her back, until his fingers moved over the slight curve of her butt. There he held her tight against him, luxuriating in the way they molded with one another.

"You fascinate me," he whispered.

She tilted her head. "Then we're even, because you're confusing me."

"I'm not a complicated man." He inhaled deeply. "I enjoy playing hockey. On Sundays I read the paper in bed. I call my family a couple of times a month and I appreciate the friends I have in my life. I'm also learning that I have a deep desire to get to know more about a woman who enjoys driving my car, has a solid dream she's determined to go after, and can go up against a room full of women without breaking a sweat."

"Dom…" She dropped her forehead against his chest.

He lifted her chin, until he could look into her eyes. "Most of all, I want to kiss you in the worst way."

"I-I can't."

She stepped back, but he pulled her closer. "Yes, you can."

"Please." She pushed against him.

He let her go, chilled from the loss of her heat and her regression. She wasn't stopping because of something he'd done or didn't do. They were having fun, getting to know each other, and she was right there with him when they danced. Whatever kept her from him came from something inside her.

"Can you tell me why?"

She slipped on his jacket, wrapping the front around her and hugging her middle. She appeared so uncertain and wary, he wanted to wrap her in his arms and never let go.

"It's…not important. I just can't." She shook her head, regret burning in her eyes.

He slipped his hands deep into his front pockets and rocked back on the heels of his shoes. Failure sat heavy on his shoulders. "It's late. We should probably go home."

She nodded. He held out his hand. Her attempt at a smile as she slipped her fingers between his broke his heart.

"I'm not going to let you run away from me without explaining. I will find out why you won't allow yourself to get closer to me before our time is up. That's a promise."

"Let it go," she said.

"I can't do that," he muttered. "For a change, I'm the one who seems to be out of control when it comes to you."

Together, they unlocked the door, walked down the stairs, and exited the empty downstairs. As the left through the back door, a flash exploded. He pulled Diana into his side, and curled her away from the paparazzi.

"Enough. You've got your picture, leave us alone." He held his hand in front of the camera and ushered Diana across the parking lot. "I hadn't realized how late we'd stayed. I think we closed the club." He held the door open as she slid into the passenger seat. "At least we got our picture taken, so we accomplished our goal."

She smiled sadly at him without answering.

He stroked her cheek. "It'll be okay."

"Will it?" she whispered.

"Yeah." He kissed her forehead. "I promise. You just have to trust me."

Rounding the back of the Porsche, he cussed under his breath. Frustrated with the inability to move things forward with Diana, he didn't have a clue what he was supposed to do to fix the situation. Couldn't she tell he liked her?

Hell, he was a walking hard-on since he'd met her. He paused outside his door, and laid his hands on the top of the car. They were both grown adults. What caused her to pull away from him?

What did she see in him that other women were blind to? It was as if life was playing a joke on him, and he couldn't have the one person he wanted. He wasn't learning a damn thing about how to fix his life, and he was taking penalty hit after hit with Diana. Life sucked.

Chapter Nine

After a silent ride home, Diana mumbled good night to Dominic and closed herself into her room. Exhausted and emotionally drained, she took off Dominic's jacket, stripped out of her dress, and stood naked, eyeing his blazer.

Without letting herself think about what she was doing, she slipped his jacket back on, covering her nakedness, and lay down on the bed. She closed her eyes, wanting to forget the fact that Dominic was close enough for her to kiss.

He'd wanted her. The hungry glaze over his eyes showed her how much he wanted to kiss her. She wanted it too, but she couldn't allow herself to go that far. She knew deep down if she kissed him, she wouldn't want to stop.

Besides, he could have anyone he wanted. All he had to do is pick one woman from the club, and he'd be having sex in his bed right now. No one ever told him no. He was a player, and he'd played her right into his arms. The whole night while they danced, she'd let herself pretend they were on a real date. She'd let herself believe that something was happening between them, that his attempt at asking her out on a date all the time and not giving up, meant something.

Everything he'd done gave her a secure feeling that he only had eyes for her tonight. Even when the other women were dressed more scantily and more beautiful than she was, he'd focused on her. She sighed. He'd done everything right. There was not one thing she could cling to that proved Dominic as a player off the rink.

God, she was in trouble.

Once she'd stopped thinking about him as a big jock, she'd seen a side of him that she found impossible to ignore. He was down to earth, easygoing, and he had an almost innocent quality about him that mystified her. A man who had women fighting over him could not possibly come away without a long track record with the ladies. All jocks were the same, and she'd been made a fool of before. Even though she'd never loved her college boyfriend in the true-adult sense, his betrayal stung her self-esteem. She rather not put herself in that same position again.

She must be missing something.

At odds with her feelings, she leaned over and picked her purse off the floor. Finding her phone, she called Shauna. If anyone could talk some sense into her, it was someone who'd loved someone famous for her whole life.

"Diana?" Shauna mumbled on the other end of the phone. "What's wrong?"

"Hey. I need your help." She rolled over on her back and sighed. "Sorry to call at this hour. I don't want you to panic, but I think I'm in trouble."

Without stopping, she quickly filled Shauna in on what happened. She even explained why she took the job and swore her to secrecy. She had no doubt her plan to buy the Ferriday house would remain between them. She could ask for no better friends than Shauna and Kate.

"Then he asked me to kiss him." She lifted the collar of Dom's jacket and sniffed. "I can't do that, although I want to. God, I want him in the worst way and it's driving me insane. I'm freaking losing my mind. I swear, you wouldn't even recognize me and the way I'm acting."

"Why?" Shauna asked. "What's stopping you from going for it with Dominic? He's a good guy, babe."

"I refuse to be another conquest in his life." She lowered her voice. "I thought this whole thing of hiring me to play his girlfriend and discovering why I wasn't attracted to him was his way of convincing me to sleep with him. I had no idea he was serious. I really thought I'd play him in his own game, but everything backfired on me. Do you know a woman tonight even pulled his hair, and we think she was hired by the cologne company that's after him?"

"That's sick." Shauna paused. "Then why did you go with him tonight if you think he's playing you?"

She snorted. "Honestly, I wanted the cash. I figured if he was stupid enough to offer, I'd be smart enough to take it."

"Oh, Diana…that's so wrong."

"I know, and I feel awful." She swallowed. "He's a professional athlete. I'm…only beginning to figure out what I want in life. The truth is, he only asked me to stay with him, because I wouldn't agree to go out with him all the other times he asked and we haven't figured out why he attracts women the way he does. I have a feeling I'm going to get my heart broken whether I make it the two weeks without having sex with him or not."

"Wait a sec. I want to ask Grayson something…"

Diana rolled over on her side, and pulled her pillow to her chest, hugging the silk pillowcase. In the background, she could hear Grayson speaking to Diana.

"Did you get that?"

"Not all of it." She sat up and crossed her bare legs.

"Long story short, Grayson said that Dominic never dates. Ever."

"No way." Diana propped her head in her hand. "He can't go anywhere without women giving him their phone number or falling over him. No man can refuse women who are openly willing to conceive his first born child in every position possible while stroking his ego."

"It's true. Grayson wouldn't lie about something like that. He goes out with women, but never has a relationship with them. Even Grayson thinks it's weird how Dominic refuses to take advantage of the women…which I'm going to punch Grayson when I get off the phone for even admitting that to me."

A man in complete control? She groaned. He was making her life crazy.

The sound of his voice, that deep timbre that left her trembling in his arms in the VIP room, rasping over her senses, had nearly been her undoing tonight. Was she wrong about Dominic?

"What am I supposed to do now?" she whispered into the phone.

Shauna laughed. "Go get laid. Isn't that what you always told me?"

"Look how that worked. You still waited to give yourself to Grayson. You were the only virgin all the way through college and even after."

"Listen. Dominic isn't like Grayson. You're not competing with anyone. There's no hurry to make up your mind tonight. You still have a couple of weeks with him. Get to know him." A slap came over the phone. "Grayson, stop."

"You two make me sick, you know that right?" Diana smiled. "I'm sorry for waking you up, go back to sleep, or back to whatever you and Grayson were doing before I called and interrupted."

"What are you going to do about Dominic?"

"Hell if I know." Diana blew her hair out of her eyes. "I'll talk to you later."

She tossed the phone to the end of the bed and flopped back on the mattress. There was nothing she could do about Dominic tonight that couldn't wait until the morning. She glanced at the clock on the nightstand and groaned. *Make that this morning.*

Chapter Ten

Despite going to bed two hours ago, Diana woke early. Biding her time, she took a bath, performed twenty minutes of yoga, and paced her room before finally opening the door and taking the chances of facing Dominic.

She peered into his open bedroom on the way down the hall, not expecting to see him lounging atop his bed in a pair of boxers reading the newspaper. Realizing she was staring, she turned to go to the kitchen when Dominic called her name.

"Yes?" She looked everywhere but at him.

"I thought you'd sleep in later after we got home so late last night."

"Habit." She shrugged. "You're up early too."

The newspaper crinkled and she snapped around to look at him. Big mistake. He'd rolled over onto his back, stretched out, and clasped his hands behind his head. *Oh. My. God.*

She couldn't help gaping at his muscular chest, the broad shoulders narrowing slightly at his waist where his boxers hung low. She gave a fleeting glance at the black boxers, and zoomed in on his thighs. *Oh, save me.*

Relaxed and looking perfectly composed, he said, "We made the paper. Someone caught us dancing in the VIP section after all. From the angle, they must've had a powerful camera and taken the shot from downstairs. Plus, they have a shot of me holding you to my chest when we exited the club."

"That's good. Your plan worked. I'm glad it wasn't a wasted evening, and you got everything you wished for."

He cleared his throat. "About last night…"

She shook her head, blinking rapidly to focus. His voice made it difficult to concentrate when he still had the rough, low timbre of sleep evident in his tone. "Yes?"

He came off the bed in one smooth move. "I wanted to apologize."

"About what?" She walked backward into the door and stopped.

"I think you're under the impression that I asked you here to get you into bed with me." He scratched his bare chest. "That you think I'm a joke…a…" He looked confused for a split second. "A player."

The tightness in her chest eased, and a dawning took shape in her mind. "Dammit. You talked to Shauna, didn't you?"

He shook his head. "No."

"Grayson?"

He grimaced. "Yeah."

"I can't believe this." She glared at him. "I suppose he told you how I hate the fact that I'm falling for your stupid charm and I worry about being just another woman in your fan club. Don't think that's gonna let you get out of paying me, because the stress alone is worth more money than you're offering me."

"He—"

"No!" She covered her ears. "I don't want to hear it. God, how embarrassing. I thought I could trust Shauna, but she's got a big mouth now that Grayson is back in her life. She shares everything with him. I'm going to kill her when I get home."

She whirled around and marched out of his room, down the hallway, and into the kitchen. First chance she got, she'd call Grayson and lecture him on the unspoken trust between girlfriends and girlfriend's fiancée. What was it with jocks? Did they have a union, swearing to tell all secrets?

Dominic followed her into the kitchen. She grabbed a mug, thankful he'd made coffee already. Ignoring him, she carried her drink into the living room and curled in the corner of the couch.

He entered the room wearing a pair of jeans only, with his own cup of coffee in hand, and sat down in the leather chair by the window. Her skin prickled, her lungs constricted, her vision blurred as she stared at the coffee table. He was like a cake in an otherwise empty house, and she was starving.

"I emailed the rep at Nomora. He'll be here in an hour." He drank his coffee as if she hadn't just made a fool of herself.

If he was willing to ignore her bout of insanity, then so could she. "Why?"

"I'm giving them their samples they need to make cologne." He managed to give her that information without giving anything away.

"I thought your point of hiring me was to keep Nomora away from you. That kind of defeats the purpose." She sagged against the couch. "Oh, I get it."

"No, I don't think you do."

She put her feet on the floor. "Hey, if you want to call this job off, fine. Give me a plane ticket, and I'm outta here."

"Stop. I don't want you going anywhere." He scooted forward and leaned over, bracing his elbows on his knees. "I thought a lot about my situation last night. If I give Nomora what they want, I'm done with them. They'll leave me alone. That's half the battle. Only the women remain, and with you being seen with me every day it's getting easier."

"Doesn't it bother you that every man will go around smelling like you?" She couldn't help snorting.

"Is that funny?"

"The world will end. Women everywhere will otherwise be occupied, chasing after all men. No one will be able to work with all the wild monkey sex going on." She laughed, and continued. "It'll be the downfall of society as we know it."

"Roles would be reversed." Dominic rubbed his hand along his jaw. "I'll be left alone."

"I doubt that." She lowered her gaze to his bare feet. Ugh, even his toes were sexy. "You just won't have as many women after you, because their interests will be divided."

"Not yours though."

She shook her head. "Nope."

"Diana—" The doorbell rang. He stood. "Shit. He's early."

"I'll get the door. You get dressed." She walked over and took his mug. When he hesitated, she leaned in and pushed him with her shoulder. "At least go put on a shirt in case they sent a woman to the house. It's too early for me to defend your virtue."

The Nomora representative who walked through the door came with a satchel of supplies he got right down to business setting up. Diana watched from the kitchen, frowning. He looked like a weasel.

Short, scrawny with a bald spot growing at each temple, his glasses hung on a too small nose. Ironically enough, he said his name was Phil. Phil Ratt, with two t's.

Sample bottles lined the table, along with tweezers, giant sized Q-tips, scissors, and a sponge. Her gaze swung to Dominic. He appeared ill, standing off to the side.

This was wrong in so many ways. For Dominic to have to sink to this level to find peace in his life was unfair. What happened to human compassion and morality?

"First thing we'll need to do, Mr. Chekovsky, is have you exercise to work up a sweat. I'll need two milligrams before we move on to the next sample." Mr. Ratt held what appeared to look like paper towels in his hands.

Dominic rubbed the back of his neck. "I can't run around the block without my security team."

"Understandable." Mr. Ratt motioned through the archway into the living room. "You could do calisthenics until we gather enough perspiration."

"Maybe this isn't a good idea." Diana stepped toward Dominic. He shook his head. "It's okay. The faster I get this over with, the sooner we can forget he was even here."

Following Dominic and Mr. Ratt into the living room, she leaned against the wall out of the way. Dominic sighed and began doing jumping jacks rather reluctantly. He kept his gaze straight ahead, not looking at her or Mr. Ratt. She clenched her teeth together.

It might not bother Dominic for Nomora to use his body for science…or cologne, but it left a bad smell in the room. Her job was to help him find answers, but this felt wrong.

After five minutes, Mr. Ratt suggested Dominic try doing a different exercise to speed up his body heat. Dominic stopped jumping, sat down on the floor, and stretched out, pulling himself into a sit up. Over and over without gasping for breath or groaning. She squinted, studying his face. He appeared no worse for wear. Not a flush on his cheeks or spot of perspiration from his forehead from all the exercise.

If someone asked her to do ten minutes of exercise, she would've perspired and collapsed on the floor. She was more a yoga girl, and believed meditation and stretching were good for the soul and balance in her life.

She glanced at the clock above the fireplace. How long would he have to exercise to break a sweat?

Mr. Ratt glanced at his watch, turned his head, and said, "He's in rather good shape, isn't he?"

"He's a Shark." She pulled her shoulders back. "No one is better at hockey than Dominic."

Dominic pushed to his feet and punched the air. One, two, added a kick, one, two. She leaned back. He was getting serious, and she wondered if he used those fighting skills to kick ass on the rink.

He caught her eye, and she almost pleaded with him to stop. Today was his day off. He shouldn't be working out, or selling his sweat. A sharp pang squeezed her heart. He looked miserable and beaten.

"Dominic?"

He spared her a glance, but kept moving. "Yeah?"

"Don't," she spoke softly. "Please."

At her pleading, he dropped his arms. Not even out of breath, he walked to her. Her heart raced. What did this man do to her? What was it about him that made her care if Nomora exposed him?

"What are you asking?" He caught one of her curls and hooked it behind her ear.

"Don't give them a piece of you. You're you, Dominic Chekovsky, and you shouldn't be marketed. You're my boyfriend, remember?" She grabbed his wrist. "We'll figure out a way to make it all go away. Together."

He seemed to study her, and then he nodded. She sagged in relief. "Thank you."

Dominic stepped around her and faced Mr. Ratt. "I'm sorry. I've changed my mind."

"B-but you can't do that, Mr. Chekovsky. My supervisors are counting on me to bring them back the proper samples." Mr. Ratt moved forward and swept the cloth down Dominic's arm.

"No." Diana rushed forward and grabbed the towel. "He said he doesn't want to be part of the study. It's time for you to leave, and if you come back without proper permission we'll issue a restraining order and take you to court for harassment."

"He's special—"

"No." She pushed the man into the other room. "He's human. That's something you all have forgotten. Now gather your things, and I'll see you out. Good bye, Mr. Ratt."

True to her word, she never left the representative's side. She shut the door, threw the lock, and inhaled deeply before turning around and facing Dominic. Standing up for him and asking him to refuse to take part in the study took their relationship to a new level. There was no going backward. She'd staked her claim, and he knew it.

The air grew thick in the house. She wouldn't be able to walk to her room without explaining why she'd blurted out her attraction to him. He'd demand answers on why she cared if he shared his scent with the world. Questions she wasn't ready to answer, because she didn't understand it herself.

It took her brain longer than it should have to realize Dominic was standing in front of her. Taken completely unaware by the predatory look in his eyes, she swallowed hard. He was against her before she could react.

His mouth hard and hot on hers. He wasn't asking, but taking. Demanding.

My God, he was scrumptious. A spicy, sensual aphrodisiac that left her putty in his hands.

He forced his tongue into her mouth, and sucked the breath right out of her. She moaned with pleasure that came from deep down in her core. His hands were rough and unyielding as they molded against the small of her back and gripped the curve of her ass. There was no room for space, even air, between their bodies as he kissed her.

She'd never seen him look so possessive. A shiver ran through her.

As he pulled back to yank his T-shirt out of his jeans, she panted. With his torso bared before her, with all of his hard heat within her reach to caress and run her tongue across, she wanted him more powerfully than she'd wanted anything in her life.

How would she ever get her fill of him? Her stomach knotted in anxiety. *It isn't possible.*

Moreover, she was the one who was going to end up hurt.

"Stop." She pushed away and cupped her elbows in her hand. "This isn't smart."

"Yes. It is." Dominic tossed his shirt behind him and reached for her again.

She shook her head. "It'd be a huge mistake. You're not right for me."

He frowned. "Why the hell not?"

"Because you have the ability to break my heart, and that's the last thing I want." She stepped around him.

"Diana…"

She shook her head without turning around and walked straight to her room.

Behind the shut door, she sank to the floor, burying her face in her hands. *I'm such a fool. He's a sports star. I'd be just another nameless woman in his past, and he'll forget about me as soon as I go home.*

Chapter Eleven

Standing in the reserved box with the other players' family and girlfriends at the Sharks arena, Diana watched the seventeen-foot shark head come down from the rafters in the middle of the rink. Metallica's song "Search and Destroy" blared over the PA system. She leaned forward, and peered around the crowd at the ice. Never having been to a hockey game, Dominic had explained what to expect on the way to the arena.

The conversation gave them something to talk about without discussing the real reason she'd kept her distance from him today. She preferred using the time at his condominium to catch up on her own life to keep the focus off her obsessive attraction to Dominic.

She'd called a realtor and made plans to walk through the Ferriday house again upon her return, and tallied how much it would cost her to redo each bedroom and update the kitchen to industrial size. For how much she wanted to forget Dominic wasn't around, she was highly aware that he paced in the living room, staying close to her the whole day without pressuring her.

The shark hit the ice, fog rolled out of its mouth, and then Dominic skated through the shark's mouth to the cheers of the crowd. She clapped, excitement taking her to the tips of her toes so she wouldn't miss a second. Warmth and pride filled her chest. She had no right to think he was hers to claim, but she was living with him and since he had no family in attendance, she'd do everything to let the fans know he had someone. Even if she was only pretending to be his girlfriend.

The music changed to the *Jaws* tune. The woman beside her nudged her arm and yelled for her to chomp. She straightened her arms out in front of her and clapped her hands in an imitation shark chomp. Laughing, she gazed over the heads of the dozen women pressed against the board and spotted Dominic.

Dominic ignored the women waving their arms to gain his attention and smiled at her. The grin on her face grew. He mouthed "chomp, chomp" back to her. She shrugged over getting caught in the excitement, never missing a beat. She couldn't help laughing. The enthusiasm in the arena was contagious. It was her first professional hockey game and she had no idea it would be this fun.

The music died away. The giant shark head went back to the ceiling of the arena, and the crowd found their seats. The woman beside her elbowed her again.

"Who are you rooting for?" The woman wrapped her scarf around her neck and slipped on a pair of mittens.

"Sharks," she said.

"No. I mean which player are you here with?"

"Dominic Chek—"

The woman grabbed Diana's arm and hugged it to her chest. "Please, please, please, introduce me to him. Please."

She pulled free of the woman. "I don't think so. He's mine."

"You're his girlfriend?"

"Yes. We're deeply in love, and I'm living with him." She lifted her chin higher. "I'm also very possessive and a martial arts master."

The woman squinted and appraised her. She glared back, not giving an inch. Tonight was as good a night as any to get the rumors started.

Finally, the woman sagged against the back of her seat. "I'm Stephanie. Bradley Keir, number fifty one, is my boyfriend."

"If you've got a boyfriend, why did you want mine?" Diana pulled the stocking cap down over her ears.

"You're joking, right?" Stephanie shook her head. "I love Bradley, but Dominic is the whole package." She sighed. "I don't have to tell you that. One look from him, maybe a nice-to-meet-you from that Russian tongue of his would last me a long time."

She couldn't argue with Stephanie's opinion. "Gotcha."

The two women in front of her whispered to each other, shot her a look over their shoulder, then leaned forward and spoke to the other row of female fans. She sunk down in her seat. At the end of the game, she feared a mob was going to break out. She should've bought a can of mace.

Three players crashed into the board in front of her. Startled, she flinched. Then she recognized Dominic as the attacker.

"Is he supposed to do that?" She scooted to the end of her seat.

"Hell yeah." Stephanie stood and yelled at the players. "Kick his ass, Dominic!"

No wonder he was in such good shape. The boxing skills he displayed yesterday in the living room came from surviving on the ice. She paid attention for the rest of the half. Learning the rules that sent a player to the penalty box, watching the way the players skate around the ice as if they knew which direction the other players were headed.

With thirty seconds left to go and the score one to one, Dominic had the puck. She stood, so she could watch him weave around two of the players on the Rangers team. She yelled his name the closer he got to the goal.

He pulled back his stick and swung. She stood on her toes and held her breath. The puck sailed past the goalie. She jumped up and down, clapping. Goal!

The buzzer rang and the players skated off the ice toward the locker room. She sat back down. Her heart raced against her chest. If no more points were made, Dominic had won the game for the Sharks. They'd have to celebrate.

"Do you want anything at the concession?" Stephanie asked.

"No, I'm good. Thanks." She shifted sideways, moving her knees out of the way.

Half the arena emptied during halftime. She crossed her legs and swung her foot with the extra room. She should've brought her phone. Shauna and Kate would've got a kick out of knowing she was actually enjoying watching a game.

Growing up, Shauna played tennis and Kate almost made a career out of cheerleading. Diana, on the other hand, never had time to play. Her parents had believed that once she turned sixteen, she would be responsible for earning her own money. Not that she begrudged their strict opinion regarding taking responsibility for herself. Their example made it possible for her to afford the Ferriday house on her own.

The money Dominic was paying her would make it possible to remodel and open for business. She rubbed her gloved hands along her thighs. The nice cushion in her bank account would see her through the first year when money was tight.

Distracted with going over her plans, she almost missed the group of women standing at the end of the aisle, staring at her. She flashed them a smile. Not knowing how long they were standing there, warmth flooded her cheeks. She probably looked like a ditz, staring off into space.

They took her acknowledgement as an invitation to approach her. She uncrossed her legs.

"We heard you were Dominic's girlfriend. Is that true?" The leader of the pack flipped her hair.

"Very much so."

"How long have you been going out with him?" She flipped her straight black hair to the other side.

If the woman kept whipping her head around, she'd get dizzy. "A few months."

"She's lying. I was with Dominic two weeks ago." A voice from the back of the group spoke. "Let me go. I'll cut the bitch."

Oh, shit. She stood. If any woman was going to fight her, she wanted witnesses. She'd scream and fight, but she wanted proof of who started the altercation so she knew whom to sue.

"Tell me, what does he whisper in your ear right before he—"

The music began. She shook her head, not hearing the rest of the question. An idiot could figure out what the woman was telling her, but she'd rather play ignorant. The women were psycho.

"He'll get tired of you." Ms. Hairwhip pointed in her direction.

"I doubt that." She raised her brows and peered down her nose. "Now, why don't you and your little entourage scurry back to your nosebleed section seats, and waste somebody else's time."

She laughed at the jaws that dropped. Ignoring them, she turned to sit down when Dominic waved her over to the bench. She walked away from the women, and went down the next aisle. Their hatred heated her back, and she wondered how much of the bitchfest Dominic had witnessed.

Dominic stood on the back of a chair and hooked his arms over the fiberglass shield. "Everything okay?"

She flipped the closest seat pad down, and climbed up until she balanced on the armrest, putting him at the right height to talk to him face to face. "Just trying to earn my money by defending your honor against one of your sleazy lovers."

"Really?" He leaned to the side and peered over her shoulder.

"I didn't get a name, but the woman you slept with two weeks ago wanted to kick my ass." She wrinkled her nose. "Really, Dom. You need better taste in women."

"I'm going to call my security team. This is going too far. I haven't—" He moved to step down, but she grabbed the sleeve of his jersey.

"I'm fine, really. We need to step it up, and put these ladies— and I use that term lightly—in their place." She stretched until she faced him nose to nose. "Kiss me, so I can save face in front of your last lover. Then go play with that little ball."

"It's a puck." He kissed her lightly on the lips. "Can I kiss you again?"

"Only if you win, big guy." She jumped down and walked to her seat.

Everyone had either returned to their seats or were making their way back to their ticket holding spot. After a quick scan of the area, she saw no sign of the women who'd bothered her. She sat down.

"I'm so jealous." Stephanie pouted.

"Don't be. You have Bradley."

Stephanie sighed. "Yes, but I still hate you for having Dominic. I always dreamed of Bradley and Dominic making a Stephanie sandwich."

"Shut up. I'm beginning to like you, and I wouldn't want to have to break your neck." Diana glared, but she softened the look by scrunching up her nose. "Any thoughts of Dominic are now mine. He's off limits to you."

Guilt flashed over Stephanie's face and told her she'd hurt the woman's feelings. Diana patted the other woman's hand. "Honey, it's time to let your fantasy go and start keeping it real. Give Bradley all the attention you can."

The next hour and a half flew by. The Sharks won three to one in an exciting game filled with fights and penalties. Diana walked up and down the aisles in the empty arena waiting for Dominic to come out of the locker room in her attempt to stay warm. Her excess energy had nothing to do with the excitement of seeing Dominic star in the game. Nope. He had enough women to show him what a superstar he was, and she wouldn't lower herself to become one of his rabid fans. She shivered. The cold coming off the rink penetrated her coat.

A bright flash blinded her to the spot. She blinked. "Who's there?"

"Thank you, Ms. Spenner," a male voice called in the distance.

She sank down in the closest seat. Okay, she was officially freaked out. She didn't sign up to be stalked by the press.

Chapter Twelve

Dominic stood in the hallway leading out of the locker room. He waited for the last few players to head out for the night before he went and found Diana. He dug the heel of his skate into the carpet. He hated to leave her out there alone, but he wanted to take tonight to reconnect with her without everyone around.

He wasn't going to take anyone's advice anymore. If she had doubts about his sincerity, he'd show her the real him.

She'd grown distant during the day, but he saw her loosening up during the game. The times he'd caught sight of her, she'd thrown herself into the Shark spirit and participated in cheering the team on. He wanted to take advantage of her good mood, and get back on solid footing again. He was on the brink of breaking through to her. He could feel it.

Whatever had made her panic when he kissed her at the condominium was no longer there when he gave her the small peck during halftime. Whether she'd been putting on a show for the females in the stands or she'd forgotten that she'd sworn against starting a relationship with him, he had no idea.

He had to convince her they were two consenting adults. He never mentioned anything about love. Not once had he asked her to love him or made it a prerequisite to the job. Hell no, he wanted to have old-fashioned wild sex with her.

Sex and love were two different scenarios. Sex left everyone feeling good and satisfied. Love was a different sport, and not for him. To shoot for love, he'd have to believe it existed. The way women threw themselves at him, he had a feeling females were worse than males when it came to putting sex before love.

The locker room door swung open. Fresnick led the remaining players out. He lifted his chin. "Good game."

Fresnick knuckle bumped him. "Are you coming to Julia's for a beer?"

"No. I have something else to do. I'll catch you next time." He took their good-natured shots at his sex life with a wink and a smile, and then headed in the opposite direction.

In the bag he carried, he'd shoved a pair of skates from the front desk that he'd borrowed before the game. He wanted to spend time with Diana, and thank her for all her help. Tonight's game had gone well, and even the coach noticed he wasn't as distracted. He'd kept his head in the game, and shot two of the three points the Sharks earned. He gave her all the credit that he played a good game.

She kept the fanatics in line on and off the rink. With her by his side, he could concentrate on his playing. Everyone was happy, and now it was time to make every effort to impress. He wanted her, and he'd do anything to prove how exploring their attraction together would be good for both of them.

He stopped inside the arena and scanned the area. Diana sat midway up the stands in the home team section. He opened the swinging door and glided out on the ice, skating to the middle of the rink.

He knew the moment she lifted her gaze and spotted him. The frown smoothed and she stood, jogging down the steps toward the board.

Motioning for her to come his way, he skated ahead and opened the referee zone's door. He stepped off the rink and pointed to the seat in front of him.

"What's up?" She approached him and sat down.

He tossed his bag on the floor beside her. "I'm taking you skating."

"On the ice?"

"That's the only place to skate."

"Get out." She laughed. "I can't skate. There's no way I could even stand up without falling."

"I'll teach you." He kneeled down and unzipped his bag. "It's easy, once you get some practice."

"I'll fall."

He smiled. "I'll catch you."

"I don't have skates." She sat down and crossed her legs. "If you want to practice more, I'll sit here and watch you."

He pulled out a pair of white practice skates. "Problem solved. Now you can go out on the ice."

"You're crazy." She sighed, shaking her head. "I don't think this is a good idea. I'm not the athletic type. It'll hurt when I fall, and what if I sprain my wrist and have to go to the hospital? My medical card is at my hotel room back in Cottage Grove."

"Then I'll pay the doctors to make you better," he said.

"Hey, the skate fits." She peered down at her foot. "How did you know what size I'd wear?"

"Lucky guess." He slipped off her other boot and smiled at the toe socks with the word Sexy splattered all over her foot. "I like you the way you are...socks and all."

He quickly laced her skates before she could come up with any more excuses. Then he stood and held out his hands. "Main thing you need to remember is to relax from your waist down. Go with the flow. If you tense, your upper body will make you lose your balance."

"Great, I'm already doomed," she muttered. "Living with you makes me tense."

"Yeah?" He stepped closer, still holding her hands. "I can help relax you before we go out on the ice."

She pushed him as her ankles careened to the side. "Whoa…"

"I've got you." He squeezed her hands, wishing the gloves she wore were gone and he could feel the warmth of her skin. "Baby steps. Don't stomp. Glide."

On the ice, her legs went one way and her upper body the other. He wrapped his arms around her and held her close, taking the weight off her legs. Her heart raced against him, clear through his shirt. She gazed into his eyes, seeking the security he could give her, and in that moment, he wanted to be the man she could depend on.

"I told you. I suck." She clutched at his shirt. "I'm not athletic… at all."

It would've been fine with him if they stood there the rest of the night with her in his arms. "Let's try something different. I'll stand behind you and hold onto your hips."

She inhaled and wrinkled her nose. "Just don't let me fall."

"Trust me." He slid into position. "I'm right here. You'll be fine."

Even with his sweatshirt covering her to her knees, he knew what was under the bulky clothes. He spanned his hands on her hips and pulled her snug against him. She molded against him, using him for support.

"Loosen your knees," he whispered into her ear. "Let me do all the work."

Slow at first, he pushed her across the ice. Halfway around the rink, her hips relaxed and he picked up speed. One full lap, she turned to gaze over her shoulder at him and lost her balance.

"I've got you." He kept going. "Have you ever roller skated?"

"Uh huh." She placed her hands on top of his. "A long time ago and I sucked at that too, but I could at least stand on my own."

"Ice skating uses the same movements. Push off with your right foot, glide, push with your left foot, glide. To start out, don't use your muscles. Just go through the motions, and I'll make sure you move forward."

"Okay." She pushed and her feet went in the opposite direction.

He lifted her by the waist, and set her back on her feet. "Again."

Again and again, she struggled to find the rhythm. He widened his stance, giving her room to move her skates. After a while, he gave her more space, never letting go of her hips. Her shapely hips. Hips that had his fingers itching to pull her back against him. Hips that teased him every time she walked across a room. He wanted more than anything to bury his head between those hips and have her scream his name.

"I'm doing it." The excitement in her voice snapped him out of dreaming about laying her down on the ice and tasting her.

He chuckled. "I knew you could."

"Okay. Okay. Hold my hand." She waved her arm out to the side. "I want to skate myself, but don't let go. Promise me."

He skated out from behind her, and linked his fingers with her gloved hand. "You're doing it by yourself, I only helped a little."

She glanced at him, wobbled, and he lifted her hand in the air until she got her balance back. "This is so fun. Let's go faster."

"Why don't we go slow." He kept her from leaning forward.

"My legs are shaking." She laughed. "I'm so out of shape."

"No, not my sweetcheeks." He squeezed her hand.

"You're so lucky I'm on the ice or I'd chase you down and make you take that back." She stared at the ice, concentrating on each step.

He skated out in front of her, skating backward, still holding her hand. "You can try. I'm right here. Come and get me."

She lifted her gaze to his, determination etched on her face. Her tongue popped out between her lips as she tried to go faster. The sight of her lips, shiny and red, caused an ache in his body. Too tempting to think about what he was doing or what he was risking, he leaned forward without hesitation or paying attention to where he was skating and kissed her.

"What are you doing?" she sputtered. "I'm going to fall."

"No you won't." He slowed down, letting her catch him, and he stole another kiss.

The adorable wrinkle between her brows grew and he couldn't help but laugh. Lust filled his brain, because it wasn't her declaration for him to stop that filled him with happiness. It was the way she puckered her lips, waiting for the next kiss when he grew close.

"You want me." He swooped in and kissed her. Longer this time. He took the extra couple of seconds to soften his lips against hers. He never gave a thought to where he skated. The rink branded in his head, he could move around the area with his eyes closed and know exactly where he was located.

"This isn't funny, Dom." She gasped.

He raised his brows and shook his head. "No. It's serious. I want you."

Before her rebuttal, he caught her with her mouth open. He kissed her again. Wrapping his arms around her back, he kept them moving and held her securely in his arms. The tip of his tongue teased hers, until she was hanging around his neck.

She kissed him back with the passion he knew she had simmering below the surface. He moved his hand upward and buried his fingers in her curls, underneath her cap, securing her head. Nothing could make him stop tasting her. Addictive and exciting, he explored her mouth with the intensity of a new game plan.

Then she demanded her own most amazing thing in a very long, very wet, very demanding way. His balls ached. His head spun, and he gave himself over to her kiss.

She moaned and he swallowed the sound, letting her pleasure fill his chest. He closed his eyes, wanting to remember every mew, nudge, and lick. His body hardened and the pressure built inside of him, threatening to burst.

Then he did burst. Right against the edge of the rink, into the boards. His feet slipped out from under him. With her in his arms, the momentum threw him off his game, and he went down. Hard. On the ice. Whether it was landing flat on his back or the weight of her body pressed on top of him, he lost his breath.

Chapter Thirteen

Diana stared into his eyes. Her vision blurred with crazy passion she'd tried so hard to ignore. She wanted him.

All of him. The adorable self-confidence he displayed on the rink. The out of this world ego that made her laugh. The determination. The strength. The funny way he tried to make her laugh with his silly nicknames.

"Please tell me to take you home and make love to you all night long." He panted underneath her on the ice.

She nodded. "I'll drive."

It seemed to take forever to get their skates off. Her fingers shook. Dominic was having his own hard time of getting them out the door and home if his constant touching her were any indication. He kissed her outside, kissed her after he helped her into the driver's seat of the Porsche, and kissed her when they'd pulled into the garage at the condominium.

Just when she had all the assurance to make love to a famous athlete, and allowed herself to relax and go with what was happening between them, he pulled back. "You understand what is happening between us, right?"

"What do you mean?"

"Sex, sweetheart." Standing in the garage, he held her an arm's length away.

She shuddered at the huskiness in his voice, the warmth in his gaze. "Dom…"

"We'll be safe." He stepped forward and nuzzled the sweet spot on her neck. "It'll be good. You'll see."

"I know." She sighed and rested her cheek against his chest.

He had no plans for her after tonight. Sure, he wanted her to finish her job, but as a girlfriend? She was just another woman in his list of lovers.

The warmth of his breath heated her skin. She'd had sex before with no strings attached. She could do it again. Besides, he lived a different lifestyle than her, and she had goals of her own that didn't involve traveling around and supporting a hockey player.

She looked up at him and smiled. "I want you too."

He swept her up and carried her into the house, down the hallway, and into his bedroom. She stretched out on the bed. His knuckles brushed her cheekbone, and brought her back to the moment. She was in bed with him. Clothed, but hopefully naked soon.

He slowly pulled her scarf out from around her neck. She shivered as the soft material skimmed her nape in the most delightful way. How could he not touch her, and have her almost begging for his hands on her body?

She leaned forward, letting him strip the sweatshirt from her. He slipped his hand into the waistband of her jeans and pulled her toward him, kissing her hard and fast. "You make it impossible to go slow." He paused. "I've wanted you ever since you ignored me in Cottage Grove, and it feels like punishment to take my time. You've been in my head for months, sleeping across the hall for days, and all I can think about is sinking myself inside of you and staying."

Validation of what they were doing came swiftly. The unsteadiness inside her vanished. "You drive me crazy."

That was the truth. She hated him for how he made her react to him. It was a constant fight to keep from falling at his feet like all the other women, but she couldn't lower herself to being like all the rest. She had to believe that this was real. There was no denying the air sizzled between them, and the way her body warmed when he was near.

He regarded her thoughtfully. "This is special. You know that, right?"

"Yes." She nodded. "And if you don't do something right this minute, I'm going to scream."

He chuckled. "I don't want you screaming…yet."

His lips brushed hers, but a wayward curl caught in her mouth. She reached to push it back and fell back flat on the mattress. He undid her jeans, and tugged them from her body, along with her panties and socks. Too hot to care about her nudity for the first time in front of Dominic, she undid the front clasp of her bra and wiggled her arms out of the straps.

He stood at the end of the bed. Without taking his eyes off her, he pulled his shirt over his head. The wide expanse of his chest left her sucking in air. Everything about him was big. Big arms, big shoulders, big chest, big thighs—she gazed down—God, those thighs.

"Too many clothes," she managed, rising on her elbows and propping herself up to watch.

In one move, he took his jeans and boxers off. She rose to her knees. Oh. My. God.

His hardness jutted out below a flat muscled stomach, proud and a little daunting. She sucked in her lower lip and clenched it between her teeth. The whole man package left her vibrating and wanting.

His strong face.

His broad shoulders.

His sculpted stomach.

His thick thighs.

She moistened her lips. His hard cock.

He joined her on the bed, both of them kneeling and facing each other. He cupped her breasts, and she had the senseless need to let her head fall back on her shoulders and close her eyes. The heat from his palms soothed and tormented.

"So beautiful," he murmured, and then nibbled her neck. "So hot."

"Yes." She slipped her arms over his shoulders. "Oh, yes."

He pushed his finger between her legs and stroked her wet heat. She trembled and sagged against him.

"Hang on, sweetheart," he whispered.

He withdrew, circled, entered, withdrew again, and gave her another circling that left her arching off the bed. He caught her earlobe between his lips, his breath tickling her senses. She shivered as her core spasmed in pleasure.

She reached down between them, and grasped his hardness with her hand, rounding her fingers and feeling the soft length of steel react to her touch. Empowered and bolder, she stroked him.

They shuddered together, each on the brink of tumbling over the edge of something wonderful.

A loud banging broke them apart. She gasped, staring at him as if he'd dosed her with a glass of ice water. He muttered a curse and jumped off the bed. Her heart raced, but not in the pleasant way it did when Dominic was touching her. Her mind couldn't connect what happened between craving more and the interruption.

She leaned over and grabbed the sweatshirt she wore earlier off the floor. "Who do you think it is?"

"Idiots." He savagely thrust his legs into his jeans. "Stay here. I'll be back as soon as I can get rid of whoever it is."

Since Dominic's sweatshirt went to her knees and covered her naked body, she ignored his orders and followed him down the hallway on bare feet. All the banging coming from the front of the condominium sounded as if someone's life was in danger, or the place was on fire and they needed to escape.

Standing behind him, she hugged her middle. He opened the door. She jumped back as two women rushed inside and threw themselves into Dominic's arms. What the...?

"Oh baby, you played a great game. Now it's time for us to show you how great of a hockey player you are." A long legged, blonde haired woman wrapped herself around Dominic.

Not to be outdone, the woman with the brassy red hair pushed her extra-large and extra-round boobs against the side of him. "It's time to celebrate your win."

Every speck of pleasure from moments ago fled and in its place, coldness filled her body. This couldn't be happening. Women really didn't show up uninvited to his house and demand sex with him, did they?

"We've got plans for you." The blonde put her lips to Dominic's ear, and spoke too low for Diana to overhear.

Disgusted and fuming, Diana planted her hands on her hips. Why wasn't he doing anything?

Not waiting for them to start peeling off his clothes and bumping uglies in front of her, she cleared her throat. The one woman with red hair spared her a glance, and went right back to trying to shut off the blood supply of Dominic's arm by squeezing his bicep between her boobs.

"Excuse me." She glared.

Dominic turned his head in her direction. Going by the roundness of his eyes, he'd forgotten she lived in his house and was almost having sex with her before the women interrupted. The fact that he looked uncomfortable now pissed her off.

"Get out!" She pulled the back of Ms. Chest's shirt, hoping the pressure would send the saline splattering all over Dominic when she busted a boob.

"Let go of me, bitch." The woman flailed her arms.

Diana, smaller and faster, dodged the manicured nails and shoved her out the door. Without missing a second, she had the blonde out the door and the lock flipped before Dominic could gain his wits about him.

She stabbed him in the chest with her finger. Twice. "I am not like those women. Do you understand me?"

He nodded. "Diana. I didn't—"

"Save it for someone who gives a shit." She marched to her bedroom and slammed the door.

Unable to breathe, she bent over at the waist and grabbed onto the dresser. The pain of almost giving herself to Dominic coupled with the knowledge it was only sex made her physically sick. Her stomach flipped and she moaned. How stupid.

It didn't matter that she'd let herself fall for Dominic. Relationships were a rare thing to him. He'd never be someone she'd be content to stay with long term. Not when he could have his choice of women, any night of the week, at his disposal. She was too good to let someone use her that way. She deserved more.

She stumbled to the bed, and lay down. Why was it when she finally let herself fall for a man, she had to pick one who would never be content with just her?

Chapter Fourteen

The next day, Dominic knocked on Diana's bedroom door. "It's almost time for practice. Are you coming?"

He couldn't blame her if she wanted to leave and quit her job. After last night, she deserved to have him hand her a plane ticket so she could go back to Cottage Grove. The situation escalated out of his control faster than he could act. He didn't want the other women. He wanted her.

Diana wrapped him in a sexual fog, not knowing what the hell he was doing at any given time. He rode high from having her beneath his fingers, hot for him. Then extreme lows when she wanted nothing to do with him.

He'd never felt such heart panging withdrawal as when she walked away from him and locked her bedroom door. Not even when he'd left Russia for the first time had he lost all sense of hope, or been this sick with worry. He had no idea how to fix everything.

He knocked again. "Diana. I'm leaving in five minutes." He paused. "I'll let you drive the Pors—"

The door opened. She stood in the doorframe, looking sexier than he'd ever seen her.

A sleeveless, lightweight black sweater clung to her curves. Soft curls hung loose around her face. A pair of skinny jeans hugged her slim legs. Black boots gave her the illusion of being much taller.

He ogled, because damned if he hadn't missed her while they slept on opposites sides of the hallway. "Do you need one of my sweatshirts?"

"No." She stepped around him and spoke while she walked to the door of the garage. "My job is to give the illusion we're dating. Since other women, strange women, aren't allowed inside the arena during practice, I'm going to go shopping while you're occupied. I'll be at the car waiting like a good little girlfriend for all your buddies to see when you come out afterward."

"Diana, I want to…" He pushed the garage door opener and walked to the car. "Never mind. Do you want to drive?"

"No, thanks. I'm good." She slid into the passenger seat.

Oh boy, he'd never seen her polite mad. Arguing mad was one thing. Hell, even ignoring mad was better than the quiet politeness she was giving him.

He climbed in the Porsche, started the engine, and backed out of the garage. Halfway down the driveway, she leaned across him and peered out the window.

"What's your security team doing here?" She'd touched his arm, before noticing and jerked away.

He gazed over at Tanner and Evan standing on the porch, before pushing in the clutch and shifting. "After last night, I called the security team and asked that they guard the house while you are staying with me. I don't want what happened to come between us again."

"It doesn't matter. Have all the women visitors you want. It's no big deal to me." She blew out her breath. "Look. I've done a lot of thinking. What happened…almost happened, won't be a problem. It was a mistake."

"Says who?" He drove out of the gate and pulled onto Doliver Street. "If you want me to believe you weren't right there in bed with me, wanting the same thing I was, then you're lying to yourself. What happened afterward, that's my fault, and I'll take the blame. But it wasn't the women who barged in on us that I wanted. It was you. It's been you since we met."

She peered out the side window, unresponsive. He drove another mile and whipped in to the parking lot of a restaurant across from the Tank. He shut off the engine.

"What are you doing?" She glanced at him.

"I want you to talk with me." He let his hands fall to his lap.

"There's nothing to say, Dominic. What happened is probably a good thing. You and I are…just wrong for each other. I'm not a prude, and I've had my share of relationships, but I won't compete with women who play unfair or with a man who can have a different woman every night if he wishes. If a man was worth fighting for, you could bet I'd die rather than let a woman put her hands on him, but you're a hockey player. The women come with the territory."

"Bullshit."

Her brows rose. "You need to respect my decision to keep this relationship as employee-employer. You knew before I agreed to the job that I had no intentions of going out with you. Living at your condominium…I let myself think something more was going on between us, when there really isn't."

"There is," he whispered, but it came out harsh and raspy to his own ears.

She shook her head sadly. "No, Dom. There's a desire to have sex together, but I won't settle for being another number to you or watching another woman take my place in your bed. It's not fair of you to ask that of me."

"What do you want from me?" He lifted his hands and let them fall on the steering wheel. "I've told you how much I care about you. I haven't been with any women for months, way before I met you. I have no control over what other people say or do. The only thing I can hope is you'll believe me."

"There are so many women—"

"In the past. None of them meant anything to me, and I know that sounds cold, but I'm not lying." He smacked the steering wheel. "How can I prove it to you when you assume the worse?"

"You don't get it. There's nothing you can do." She sagged against the seat. "You're going to be late for practice."

"Screw practice." He opened the door and walked out into the breeze.

Frustrated, he wanted to kiss her into accepting them together. Her reasons made no sense. Why deny what they felt when they were together if they were both having a good time?

He stepped over onto the sidewalk and leaned against a palm tree, facing the Pavilion. Coach would kick his ass when he showed up late for practice.

His tardiness would probably put another check mark by his name on reasons why he should be traded. It didn't matter where he went, whether it was the Detroit Red Wings, his old team, or a new team, the women were everywhere, and Diana was lost to him.

Maybe fighting for what he wanted wasn't even worth it anymore. He could play hockey in Russia, and he missed fitting in with everyone else. Yet, he loved the United States. Both places left him floundering to find contentment. His love of hockey was the only bright spot to getting up in the morning. There had to be more to life in the off hours.

"Dominic?" Diana called his name.

There was no judgment in her voice, and no hostility, or anger. Maybe a little curiosity and regret, but that could be his mind playing tricks on him. Lately, he seemed to be imagining a hell of a lot.

She stood outside the Porsche with her hand shielding her eyes from the glare of the sun. His breath caught in his chest. Was he supposed to let her go now? Give up before he even had all of her?

The thought of never seeing her again wasn't acceptable. He wasn't ready to give up on them. If he could figure out why he fought so hard to bring her into his life, maybe he could figure out why he wanted her to stay.

Trying to figure out why Diana had the power to stay away from him when other women failed still eluded him. If he couldn't have her, then his object to straighten out his own life was one big fucking failure.

He shoved his hands deep into his front pockets and strolled back to the car. She watched him with a curious gaze as he walked to the driver's side. He paused at the door, looking over the roof of the car at her.

"I don't know what to say to you. I only know I don't want you to leave me yet. Will that be enough?"

She studied him, seeming to come to her own conclusions. Finally, she glanced away and nodded. "I'll stay and finish my job."

He swallowed. *Good.*

Five minutes later, he walked into the arena after handing the keys to the Porsche to Diana. Coach Gunderson stood at the skate walk through. Dominic slowed his pace and approached him. Shit. He was in trouble.

"Dammit, Chekovsky." Coach's voice boomed. "Get suited and out on the ice. That's your last warning. If you're late again, your ass will be on the bench and I'll fine you."

"Yes, Coach." He hustled into the locker room.

He had to get his shit together. It'd take nothing for the Sharks to trade him, even though he was the captain of the team. Bad publicity and troubles were frowned upon and he had a ton of them riding his back. Instead of going down in a storm of chaos, he'd quit first. It was that simple. He had to find out why he attracted women to him before he ruined his career. The last thing he wanted to happen was the disarray of his life to force him to give up on playing hockey in the States. The one thing he was capable of loving.

Chapter Fifteen

Two hours later, Diana drove into the arena's parking lot after going window shopping nearby. The stores remained a blur, because she'd thought about Dominic the whole time she wandered the shops. It wasn't her imagination. Something else besides their flubbed up attempt at sex bothered Dominic.

His troubles went beyond the stress of the women fans and his inability to find peace in the United States. For a moment while they were discussing their situation in the car, he'd allowed her to see the pain he was going through. Part of her wanted to believe she was causing the vulnerability he was showing, but the odds were not in her favor.

Who was she? Before coming here, she'd known nothing about hockey. She spent her time working, saving money, and on Fridays, she'd participate in Girls' Night Out with Shauna and Kate. That's it. She had goals to run a B & B, not tie herself down to a man who traveled the States playing hockey with hundreds of women at his disposal.

Yet, she couldn't deny her attraction. The way she looked forward to spending time with him, even when she was trying so hard to make him leave her alone. She opened the door of the Porsche and stepped outside. Okay, a big part of her liked how he never gave up. It was like having a big sexy stalker.

What woman minded having that kind of problem?

A car pulled in beside her. She leaned against the Porsche. Irritation surfaced.

Four women piled out of the vehicle, giggling and messing with their hair. She rolled her eyes. No doubt, they were here for Dominic. The extreme positivity that they'd succeed in landing the hockey star threatened to choke her with jealousy.

Oh, damn. She turned around and leaned her head against the car. She was jealous.

That emotion should never come out unless she envied what someone else had. Yet, the boiling hatred for them was alive and well inside of her. Those women had no tie to Dominic, except for their undying love they hoped he'd return to them. She knew without a doubt Dominic didn't love the attention. He'd told her many times. She'd seen it with her own eyes.

She straightened, cast a glance over her shoulder, and then headed toward the arena. Those bitches were not going to get her man.

The faster she walked, the more determined she became to make sure they stayed far away from Dominic. She had a week and a half left with him, and she wasn't going to blow an opportunity to experience being with him on her ability not to loosen up. Someday, when she was old, gray, and rocking on the porch of her Bed and Breakfast, she'd regret not having sex with him.

The front door of the arena swung open. Hearing the women behind her gaining ground, she jogged up the steps. Dominic spotted her right away. In the time it took her to scale the top step, she'd come to a firm decision. She was going to sleep with Dominic.

He only had eyes for her. The other women were not even spared a glance from his icy gaze. She wanted more than anything to keep his attention. She jogged across the landing.

He dropped his bag, and she sailed into his embrace. She wrapped her arms around his neck. "I'm sorry," she whispered. "I'm a mess. I didn't mean to make this more complicated."

"You're the sanest woman I know." He leaned in and placed his forehead against hers. "God, I thought I lost you and you were going to leave without giving us a chance."

Their breath mingled. A smile spread across his face, and she laughed. She'd seen that look before. A rush of complete rightness unlike anything she'd ever experienced left her shaking.

"Pucker, sweetheart, because I need to k—"

She captured his lips. Hard, insistent, and passionate. When she'd nibbled, sucked, and stroked her tongue against his, she leaned back, fully satisfied with herself.

He cupped her face between his hands. His thumbs swept her cheeks. Then he leaned in, slid his nose along hers, and lifted her face up as he brought his face down and kissed each cheek.

"I'll need more than that." He brushed her lips. "You can't kiss me and leave it unfinished."

"Unfinished?" she murmured.

He nipped her bottom lip. "Uh huh."

Not stopping, he kissed the tip of her nose. She closed her eyes, and she felt his warm lips on her eyelid, and then the other lid. She clutched on to the front of his shirt, not trusting her legs to keep her standing.

"I want…" He placed his mouth on hers, softening the kiss. "More."

"But what happens—"

"We'll go slowly." He hugged her to him. "Let's go out on a date. A real date. Tonight. Okay?"

She held onto his hand and went with him down the steps. The women approached and Dominic totally ignored them. She squeezed his fingers. How could she deny that he never paid the other women any attention? Even last night, when the women hung on him, he'd stood stiff and uncomfortable.

Once they settled in the Porsche and took off from the arena, Diana asked him to let her out in front of a small boutique. She ran inside while he sat in the car. He'd already seen her in her little black dress, and she wanted something special. Not one to splurge, being away from home forced her to use the emergency money she kept in her purse. Tonight called for something so freaking fantastic, Dominic would remember her for a long, long time.

Before she talked herself out of the outfit she'd spotted earlier, she tried it on, smiled into the mirror in satisfaction, and quickly told the sales woman she'd take the dress.

A half hour later, back at home, she shut herself in her bedroom and got ready for the evening. Nervous and excited, she went all out in the primping department.

She took a bath, painted her nails and toes, toweled her curls and let them dry naturally. She went darker on her makeup, spritzed her body, and then slipped into her new outfit. At the bedroom door, ready to go out and join Dominic, her phone rang, stopping her on the spot.

Being away from Cottage Grove, she knew she had to answer. She read the screen. *Kate*.

"Kate, what are you doing?" She walked over to the edge of the bed and sat.

"Better question. What the hell are you doing with Dominic Chekovsky? Shauna's here and she just told me you're staying with him for two weeks, and you didn't call me."

"It happened fast. We had to get out of town before Dominic caused a scene like last time he came to Cottage Grove. Plus he's playing in season," she said. "He's got practice all the time, and then there's the games. He's a busy guy."

"Look at you, talking hock-lish." Kate laughed. "Listen. Are you going to make it back next Friday?"

She hadn't even thought about when she was going to return. That was only five days away. That's all the time she had left with Dominic? The thought depressed her. "Yeah. I don't know when

Dominic is going to fly me home, but I'll be there sometime that day. Why?"

"Bruce, Crista, and Juan are coming into town. Shauna and Grayson want us all to get together at the Quay. Also, Crista is staying at the hotel and wanted me to tell you she expects you to come. She said you can bring the big guy with you too." Kate dropped the phone. "Sorry."

Grayson's friends came to help in the fundraiser, and had become friends with all of them. Bruce was a world-class professional bass fisherman. Crista had won first place in the Ironman marathon, and was training to participate in the next one set in Hawaii. Juan, the sexy flirt, was a professional skier in the Winter Olympics.

"If I make it back in time, but I'll be alone. Dominic won't be coming back with me, since he's got a game," she said.

Kate groaned. "Oh, before I forget. Your dad wants you to call. He approached Shauna and ended up lecturing her about you going on vacation and blowing your hard earned money."

She dropped her chin to her chest. "Okay. I'll give Dad a call tomorrow and talk with him. Tell Crista I'll be home and I can't wait to see her again."

"Hey, you okay?"

"Yeah. The job with Dominic is harder than I thought…"

"What's going on?" Kate asked.

"Oh nothing. Just putting myself out there to be hurt in the end." She snorted. "Shauna can fill you in. Tell her I gave my permission. But to sum it all up, I want Dominic."

"But you hate him."

"I used to, but—" A knock came from the door. "Shit. I have to go." She stood and inhaled a deep breath. "I'll call you tomorrow."

"I hate when people don't tell me what's going on," Kate said.

She smiled, because she knew her friend was a social butterfly and demanded to know all the gossip first hand. Being engaged to the son of the town's richest family took Kate to high places and she lived for the excitement. "I need to go. I'll talk to you later."

"Wait!" Kate paused. "Are you sleeping with him yet?"

"No."

"Remember to make him wear a condom. Be smart." Kate laughed. "Have fun. I bet he has a huge—"

"Goodbye, Kate." She pushed the disconnect button on the phone.

She shook her head in amazement. Count on her friends to boost her when she needed someone to tell her she was doing the right thing and not making the biggest mistake of her life.

"Diana?" Dominic knocked again.

"Yeah, coming." She wrinkled her nose. Bad choice of words, considering she was talking about sex with Kate seconds ago.

She opened the door. Every butterfly that'd stayed dormant her whole life picked that moment to flutter. Her nipples peaked and she swallowed her nerves.

The smile washed from Dominic's lips and he whistled. Dressed in a white silk dress shirt, black tie, and black slacks, he stood with his arms loose, his hands in his pockets. "You're beautiful."

"Thanks," she said, happy she'd splurged on the red curvy dress. "You look incredible."

He leaned over, and paused. "May I?"

"You better. I'm nervous." She tilted her face.

Gentle and slow, he pressed a warm kiss upon her lips. He studied her before taking her hand and leading her through the house. Tonight's date held mystery and anticipation. They were no longer pretending.

"I hope you're ready. I planned a big night for us." Dominic held the garage door open, and she stepped ahead of him.

"What about your game tomorrow? Shouldn't you have an early night?" She stood beside the Porsche.

He shrugged, opening her door. "It'll be fine. Once I load up in the morning on carbs, I'll be ready to play."

Once they both buckled their seatbelts, Dominic pushed the garage opener and started the car. She could get used to thinking she was first in Dominic's life.

Halfway down the driveway, red and blue lights lit up the interior of the car. Diana turned to Dominic, but before she could question where they came from, her body pitched forward against the shoulder restraint as he slammed on the brakes.

Dominic peered in the rearview mirror, then whirled around and gazed out the back window. "What the hell?"

She followed his line of vision and gasped.

Three police cars blocked the end of the driveway. A crowd formed beyond the cruisers, and Dominic's security team jogged toward the Porsche.

"What happened?" She reached for his hand.

He frowned. "I don't know, but I'm going to find out."

Chapter Sixteen

Dominic wanted to punch someone.

"Go back inside, and we'll work on crowd control." Officer Patrickson nodded in the direction of the condominium. "We'll clear the area."

He clamped his teeth together. The reason he'd bought the condominium was for the gated security. "I want to know how they broke through the security measures. That's twice in one week this has happened."

"From what we're gathering, these are all women from your community." Officer Patrickson removed his bully club. "The sooner you go inside and out of sight, we'll take care of the matter and send them home."

He turned around, disgusted at having his private space invaded. All the inexcusable behaviors of these women shaded his attitude toward others. Plus, it just plain pissed him off.

"Dominic?" Officer Patrickson slapped his hand over his shoulder. "Good luck tomorrow in the game. Me and a couple of the guys have tickets and will be cheering you on. I have a hundred bucks riding on you scoring three of the points."

"Thanks," he replied, shrugging him off and heading toward Diana.

Diana stood in the driveway, staring out at the other women. Quiet and alone, he suspected she was finally finished with him. He couldn't expect her to understand and accept his lifestyle. It wasn't fair of him to expect her to deal with the attention and always having their time interrupted by the bullshit that came with him everywhere.

He approached her. "The officers want us to go inside. I'm sorry."

"It's not your fault." Her voice soft and understanding made the situation worse, and the guilt he was feeling burned like acid in his stomach.

He led her back toward the garage. In front of the Porsche she stopped.

He leaned over and gazed into her eyes. "What's wrong?"

"Someone's in your car," she whispered.

"Stay here." He left her standing there, jogged over to the car, and peered through the driver's window. A definite shadow took shape behind the darkened window. "Dammit."

He opened the door. Mr. Ratt from Nomora sat in the driver's seat, swabbing the steering wheel. "Get out."

When Mr. Ratt hesitated, Dominic grabbed him by the front of the shirt and hauled him out of the vehicle. He pulled him over and slammed him against the hood. "Leave me alone."

"B-but Mr. Chekov—"

Dominic punched him in the gut and let go of him. Mr. Ratt slumped to the ground, groaning and sucking in air. Someone grabbed his arm, and pulled him back.

"What's going on?" Officer Patrickson stepped between them, his hand on Dominic's chest.

"He's trespassing." He fisted his hands at his sides. "I want him arrested."

Officer Patrickson forced Mr. Ratt to his feet, turned him around, and handcuffed his arms behind his back. Dominic fumed as he paced beside the car. This had to stop.

"Wait." He approached Mr. Ratt. "I'll let you take whatever you were touching in my car." He loosened his tie, ripped the buttons off his shirt, removed it, and wiped the material against his armpits. Then he handed Mr. Ratt the clothes. "Take it all."

"Dominic…no." Diana slipped her warm arm around his bare waist. "Let the police arrest him. He can't invade your privacy this way. It's wrong."

"With the police officer as a witness, do you swear you'll leave me alone now?" Dominic glared at Mr. Ratt who nodded. "If you don't, the next time you step on my property or trespass or try to steal my belongings, I'll have you arrested. I'll be filling out a restraining order tomorrow. I'm done dealing with Nomora and you."

"Yes, s-sir." Mr. Ratt held the clothes away from his body. "You gave us everything we need."

"Are you asking me to let him go? Because we have enough to charge him for trespassing and intent to steal," Officer Patrickson said.

"Get him out of my sight and make sure he doesn't come back. I'll be in soon to file the restraining order." He ran his hand through his hair. "Get them all the hell out of here."

Diana never left his side. Instead, she urged him with gentle pressure against his back toward the house. In the kitchen, he opened the cabinet above the fridge and removed a bottle of tequila. Like everything else in his life, tonight had ended up differently than he'd expected.

She held out her hands. "Here. Give it to me. I'll pour you a drink."

He passed the bottle to her. She carried it over to the counter, found two shot glasses, poured liquid into each cup, and carried the drinks back to him. He tilted his head and looked at her. Really looked.

She'd accepted the change in plans without snapping his head off or causing a scene. Outside, she'd stayed away from the crowd rather than fly to his protection the way she did at the game or on their pretend date. Yet, she'd tried to protect him against Nomora.

"Thank you." He clinked the glass against hers.

She smiled softly. "For what?"

"Just being here, and not walking away. For keeping your cool when I was losing mine." He stared down into the shot and swirled the clear liquid. "It means everything to me."

"I want to be here for you," she said.

He raised his gaze and caught her licking her bottom lip. What he saw endeared her to him. She was strong and independent but when it mattered, she stuck by his side.

They raised their glasses at the same time. He swallowed in one gulp. The burn hit him instantly and he blew out his mouth. Diana reached out and gripped his forearm, held her breath, her eyes watering.

He grinned. "Breathe."

She let out her breath in a big rush and coughed. "Oh. My—" She coughed again. "God, that burns."

How pathetic they'd turned out. Hiding in the kitchen, dragging down tequila, and pretending everything about tonight was normal when it definitely was not.

"One more." He moved over and brought the bottle back with him. "To our first official date."

"But we haven't gone out." She laughed.

He held up the glass. "I'm not admitting defeat yet. I won't let anyone ruin tonight. Drink up."

Diana handled the next shot better. He took the glass from her hand and led her into the living room. He stood her in the middle of the room, and motioned for her to stay there. "I'll be right back. Don't move an inch."

He had no experience with dating or trying to impress a woman, so he ran on instinct. He docked his iPod into the sound system and turned the music on low. A melody filled the house, and he smiled. Perfect.

What else? He studied his room. Date. Date. Date. Crap.

He had no idea what normal people expected to do when they stayed inside together, except have sex and he wasn't ready to press Diana too fast. They'd already danced on their first pretend date. That was fun. Well, more than fun. He wanted her in his arms again, but dancing was too obvious. No, he had to come up with something much better than dancing or cooking her dinner.

"Dominic? What are you doing?" she called from the other end of the condominium.

Groaning and out of time, he grabbed two hockey sticks leaning against the corner of his room and one of the folded jerseys off the top of his dresser. Halfway down the hallway, he remembered sports socks. Prepared to do the only thing he was confident in, he returned to the living room with his arms full.

Diana eyed him curiously. He tossed her his jersey. "Go change your clothes. I'm challenging you to a game of sock hockey."

"What?" She laughed. "Never heard of it."

He smiled. "I'll teach you how to play, but I don't want you ruining your beautiful dress. I want you to wear that when I can take you out properly and show you what normal is."

"I have my own clothes. I don't need your shirt."

"No." He lowered his voice. "I'm skins." He slapped his bare chest. "You'll be shirts."

"Does this have to do with your kink of seeing me in your clothes?" She covered her mouth to hide her grin, but failed. Her eyes twinkled with laughter.

He sat down on the couch and began to untie his shoes. "It has everything and nothing to do with what I want. Now hurry. Five more minutes and you forfeit the game."

Her laughter followed her through the house and out of sight. He took off his dress socks, and put on his sports socks. Then he got busy clearing the room and shoving all the furniture up against the walls. Last, he rolled the Persian rug and stood the bundle in the corner of the room.

He looked at the area, himself, the white socks sticking out from under his black slacks, and had a second thought about his plan. God, he hoped he wasn't making a fool of himself.

Diana cleared her throat. He turned, and the room swayed.

Wearing his jersey and nothing else, she posed at the edge of the room. His shirt hit her above the knees. Normally the short sleeves covered his biceps but on her, the T-shirt covered her down to her wrists. The V-neck plunged between her breasts, and he knew she had something on underneath because her black bra peeked through the mesh. He dropped his gaze and all the blood in his body pounded. The thinnest black strap along her hip showed through the white material. He had no idea if she was aware of how transparent the breathable material was, but right now he was thankful he played for the San Jose Sharks and gave her one of the jerseys he wore on away games.

"Is this how you wanted me?" She walked on bare feet into the room.

He failed at swallowing. Unable to voice an answer, he stood there staring with his mouth open.

Chapter Seventeen

Her own lust reflected back to her in Dominic's gaze. She would never get used to seeing him bare chested and looking at her as if the very touch of her would set him on fire. He gave her confidence to go through with wearing his jersey. She knew he could see through it when she stood with the light from the hallway behind her.

"You're not saying anything." She pointed her thumb over her shoulder. "Should I go change?"

"Hell, no. Please don't." He seemed to snap out of staring at her. "Come in."

She walked slowly, enjoying the way his gaze followed her legs across the room. His reaction made her daring and bold, suddenly glad she'd skipped the sweats and decided to risk it all.

"Sit down." He held her hand and lowered her to the floor.

He followed her down and pulled her foot onto his lap. "You need the right equipment if you're going to play with me."

"Play with you?" she whispered, clearing her throat. "I give you the green light and you don't hesitate, do you?"

"I'm not stupid," he whispered back.

The thick white tube socks Dominic pulled over her toes tickled her feet. She squirmed, and glared at him when he laughed.

"I've found your weakness." He slid the socks slowly up her leg, past her knees. "Mm…"

She shivered. The contrast of such a big man who fought on the rink for a living who was able to handle her with tenderness appealed to her.

His almost boyish fascination with the female body confused her. He acted as if he'd never seen a woman's bare skin before. She flinched as he worked the other sock onto her foot, then relaxed as he reached her ankle. If she met him today, and had no idea about his rather unique lifestyle, she'd swear he was some normal guy who got lucky in the looks department. And the body department. She sighed. Personality department too.

"There you go." He left his hand on her knee. "You're ready for sock hockey."

"What in the world is that?" She pushed off the floor and stood.

"It's how I learned to play hockey." He grabbed the extra pair of socks and pushed himself to a standing position. "Back in Russia, when I was little, my father would take me down to the basement where he'd cleared out the whole room. He'd hand me an old stick, usually a broken broom, that he'd taped a book onto the end—" He held up the rolled pair of socks. "Then we'd use a taped ball made out of old socks as the puck. It was in that basement where I spent my childhood, playing hockey against my father."

"Oh," she whispered.

His mouth softened. "My mother would sit on the stairs and keep score. Sometimes, she'd make us sosika…um, hotdogs, and splurge on kvas, which is like your soda. She liked to make a big show of me winning."

"It's a happy memory for you." She smiled. He'd lapsed back into a thick accent.

"Very much so. A time in my life I bury deep in my heart, because my parents were my life and I keep those times hidden and untouched." He shrugged. "I usually never talk about my childhood to others."

"Why not?"

He inhaled deeply and breathed out his nose. "It's a memory for me alone. My family brings me comfort, and I keep them to myself so no one can ruin my happiness."

"Why did you share it with me?"

He leaned over and kissed her lips. "Because I wanted to."

She blinked rapidly. Touched that he thought so much of her to share a part of him he kept heavily guarded from others, she cleared her throat. "You miss them."

He nodded. "Yes, but I don't want to go home. I love America, and I get to help my family more if I am playing hockey here. That's important to me."

"You send them money?" She waved her hand in the air. "Never mind. That's none of my business."

"It's okay for you to ask me anything. Yes, I give them money, but that only brings me comfort in knowing I'm making their lives more enjoyable. The real reason I stay here and play is that it brings pride to my family name for them to have a successful son. It's how they become the richest family in our village. It's not about money, but that I have succeeded in America that brings honor to them," he said.

"That's why you hired me, so you can be happy here while making sure your family stays proud of you." She pushed the sleeve of the jersey higher.

He nodded. "Yes."

Everything about Dominic made sense. His reluctance to have a meaningful relationship in the crazy life he found in America. His hatred for the disturbances from all the women who threatened his livelihood, and in a way, his family. She blinked away the moisture gathering in her vision. He really did need her. He wasn't lying.

"Okay. Let's get playing then." She clapped her hands together and shook off the sentimental feelings welling in her chest. "What are the rules?"

He walked over and picked up the hockey sticks, handed her one, and dropped the makeshift puck on the floor. She eyed the plastic casing on the bottom of the stick, glad to see something along the edge. She wouldn't want to mar his wood floors.

"If I get the puck to the hallway, I get a point." He hitched his thumb over his shoulder. "You must get past me and have the puck hit the couch for you to score."

She eyed the playing field. "That's easy enough."

He laughed and shook his head. She crossed her arms. Hockey might not be her sport, not that she had one to call her own, but she knew how to play against men.

"You're so going down," she said.

"Keep your stick low to the floor. We don't want your legs getting bruises." He dropped the bundle of socks, and pushed it into the middle of the room. "Besides those rules, anything goes."

"Anything?" She grinned.

He arched his brow. "Bring it on, sweetcheeks."

A challenge. She posed with her stick beside the puck the same way she'd seen him do it many times during practice and games. He might have a skill and be bigger than she was, but she wasn't without tricks of her own.

"Three."

"Two."

"One."

He hit the sock between her spread feet, moved around her, and hit a long shot into the hallway. She remained in position, gazing over her shoulder. He was fast. She'd give him that much.

Chekovsky 1, Spenner 0. He grinned.

"I wasn't ready." She pulled the front of the jersey away from her body and leaned over when he returned. Without looking, she knew her shirt hung low and open. If he wanted, he could look straight down her body.

She stayed bent over at the waist and peered up at him. "This is fun."

His gaze dropped. She almost laughed. It was too easy.

"Three, two, one," she blurted, hitting the puck to the left.

He hesitated and she beat him to the bundle of socks. She squealed as he bore down on her and lost control of where the puck went. He swung and she watched the white blob sail into the hallway as he made another goal.

She'd have to step up her game. It was time for operation sexy.

Without missing a move, she stretched her arms over her head, holding the stick in the air. She twisted side to side at her waist. The material of the jersey skimmed her butt, and going by Dominic's state of hypnosis, he got a peek of her underwear.

"Go!" She lowered her arms, flicked the sock to the right, and swung. The puck bounced off the couch. "Score!"

She stuck the stick between her thighs, held out her arms, and performed the chomp, chomp, chomp. To rub it in, she then danced around in a circle.

Dominic groaned and pointed to the floor in front of him. "You want to play tough, let's make the stakes higher. I get the next point…I get to kiss you."

"Fine." She tossed her hair. "And what do I get if I win?"

He winked. "Anything you want."

"Deal." She widened her stance, positioned her stick, and wiggled her ass. "Do it."

He dropped the puck.

A clattering of wood against wood commenced as they dueled with their hockey sticks. She laughed, gasping when he nudged her back with his hip. She wrapped one arm around his waist without giving up. Her breath came in pants through her laughter.

Dominic shifted and hugged her face first into his chest. Blinded, she dropped her stick. She stepped on top of his feet, and he walked the length of the room with her riding along and hit the puck down the hallway.

"I win." He dropped his stick and tilted her face toward him. "Pucker up, sweetheart."

She stared at his mouth, at his lips, and realized she'd thought about kissing him again at least a hundred times since the last time they touched. In an instant, everything fell away, including her socks that slipped down her legs and puddled around her ankles.

He captured her lips, pulling her body to him. My God, he was delicious. Powerful, endearing, and satisfying.

He nudged her mouth open, slipped his tongue inside, and turned her knees to putty. Deep down, she knew that Dominic would give her pleasure no matter what they were doing.

All she wanted to do was immerse herself in him. Let the sensations whipping through her body carry her wherever he wanted her to go. For tonight, for their brief time together. Then she could go on with her life and remember this moment.

She'd hold on tight to the man who'd danced with her when it was obvious he had no idea what he was doing. She'd remember the boy who recreated the game of sock hockey to share his family with her. She'd never forget him, no matter what happened tomorrow.

Then when her time with Dominic ended, she'd learn how to be strong again and go after her own dream that much richer for knowing such a wonderful man.

For now, she was lost and there was no stopping. He lifted her closer, moving with her, the hard length of his erection pressed firmly against her.

"So sweet," he whispered as he nibbled her bottom lip. His teeth tugged, his tongue licked over the gentle bite as she wiggled against him, wanting him to touch her all over.

She sought his kiss again, her head tilting, her tongue licking at his lips. A moan shuddered from her chest as he gave her what she asked. Hot and determined, he ravaged her.

Oh God, she was going to embarrass herself by throwing him to the floor and pouncing on him. How had she lasted this long living with him right across the hallway without ending up in his bed?

He picked her up without taking his mouth off her. She circled her arms around his neck, making sure he wouldn't stop or let her go.

Halfway down the hallway, the doorbell rang. She pulled her mouth away and groaned. "Please, make them go away."

He kept walking to his room, through the door, and placed her on the bed. The doorbell rang again. Dominic paused. She closed her eyes and sighed. Freaking…unbelievable.

"Go. Just go." She rolled over and hugged his pillow to her chest. Even to her own ear, she heard the pathetic sound of failure coming from inside of her.

Chapter Eighteen

Diana stood against the wall outside the locker room at the arena, her arms folded, her eyes on the floor, and her mind fleeting from her thoughts about Dominic to her life when she goes back to Cottage Grove. She couldn't make sense of anything. All her nerves were bundled and tight. She couldn't focus. If she held her hand up in the air, she was sure it would be shaking.

The effects of not having sex and being highly turned on were starting to wear her down.

Last night, Officer Patrickson had returned and after taking a statement, he'd cajoled three tickets for today's game out of Dominic for more of his friends to attend the sellout game between the Sharks and the New York Rangers.

By the time he came to bed, she'd fallen asleep. The big idiot didn't wake her, but crawled in beside her and held her all night. She hated herself for not noticing or waking up. She'd slept like a baby, and woke up late, wanting Dominic in the worst way.

During the ride to the game, they barely kept their hands off each other but they were running late, because they both overslept. In addition, the game lasted freaking hours, plus two overtimes. Time they could've been using in other ways. Once she made up her mind to sleep with him, she became impatient. They could be at the condominium making love right now.

Waiting for him to shower and exit the locker room had her complaining with the other girlfriends and wives that waited for their husbands or boyfriends. She sighed heavily. Five more minutes, and she was going to walk into the showers and drag Dominic out.

Stephanie studied her from the other side of the hallway. She'd tried to ignore the other woman. When that didn't work, she walked over and joined her. "Good game, huh?"

"Yep. They'll be celebrating tonight. Are you coming over to Julia's?" Stephanie shifted her purse to the other arm. "Everyone's coming. I bet the guys would like if their captain showed up."

"Does he usually?"

Stephanie nodded. "At least before you moved in with him, he did."

It wasn't only her life tipped upside down when she'd agreed to Dominic's job offer. He'd rearranged his life too.

"We might go. I'd have to ask Dominic first. Sounds fun." She tried not to sound flippant, but a night surrounded by the other women was not on her list of things to do during her stay.

Stephanie laughed. "Don't worry. The talk around the arena is everyone has dropped their lust filled crushes on your boyfriend."

"Huh?" She stood straighter. "What's that mean?"

"You didn't notice that no one paid him any attention tonight?" Stephanie shrugged. "He's taken."

"Wait." She turned and faced her directly. "You're telling me that no one is going to hit on Dominic anymore? We're free to go out in public without being mobbed?"

"Yeah. Who wants a guy who is in love with another woman? I don't. No woman does." Stephanie pushed off the wall. "He's all yours."

She stared after Stephanie. When did all that happen? Last night, even the women in his gated community had come over to try to gain a moment of private time with Dominic. She gazed around at the others. Tonight, no one spared her a glance.

No glares. No evil eye aimed her way. No hostile takeover. No mental plots to plan her demise.

She smiled. *We did it.*

Their plan to pretend to be boyfriend and girlfriend worked exactly the way Dominic wished. She bent her knee and tapped the heel of her shoe against the wall. He'd be thrilled with the changes in his life, and she'd go on to be the owner of the new bed and breakfast in Cottage Grove.

Pleased and satisfied with their accomplishment, she couldn't wait to tell him. She wouldn't even have to spend the last week with him. She stilled. Her stomach knotted, and she let her head fall back against the wall. Their time together would end. She'd have to leave him.

The thought of never seeing him again, or worse, seeing him every time he flew into Cottage Grove to visit Grayson and knowing he wasn't coming to be with her, pained her. She couldn't handle seeing him, knowing he was going away again and there would be a woman waiting for him whenever he lifted a finger.

She had no doubt that the mass hysteria that followed him everywhere might end, but she'd bet the half million dollars Dominic was paying her that he wouldn't stay alone for long. He was the whole package and some woman would see through his ego to the real man inside.

He had more money in the bank than he could spend. She swallowed. For God's sake, he sent money home to his parents. What kind of man did that? It went against everything her father drilled into her head. She was responsible for her own success, no one else, yet Dominic shared his security with others. That fact alone amazed her.

He remained positive even when life treated him roughly. She rubbed her arms. He put socks on their feet and played hockey in the living room with her. He'd gone overboard to make sure he made up for her disappointments and in return, endeared her to him.

She even daydreamed about how they could make a relationship work. They could make their home in Cottage Grove. He could use a charter plane to get to practices and games. Or she could hire a manager at the B & B, and stay in San Jose with him during the season.

"Oh my God," she whispered. Why was she planning a future with him?

Dominic approached her. "Hey."

Since meeting him, she hadn't wanted to stop living life to the fullest. She wanted to experience everything. And she wanted to do it with him.

"What's going on?" He caressed her cheek with the back of his hand. "You look upset."

She grabbed his hand. "We're going to Julia's with your teammates."

He frowned. "I thought we'd go home. Maybe finish what we keep starting and getting interrupted doing."

"We have time. Tonight, I want to experience your life, what you do when I'm not here. Let me see how you celebrate a win." She leaned forward and kissed him quickly. "Please?"

He studied her. "Okay. Sure."

"Great." She wrapped her arm around his waist. "Good game, by the way."

"Thanks," he mumbled, taking her hand and leading her out the door to the car. "Are you sure you don't want to go home? I was looking forward to celebrating the big win and finally having you underneath me. Nothing is going to stop us tonight, I promise."

She kissed him. "The night's not over, big guy. We have time. That I promise you."

On the way to Julia's bar, Dominic pulled over at a gas station. He took off his seatbelt, leaned over, and kissed her. She almost changed her mind about going out with the other guys on the team.

Six blocks later, Dominic stopped the Porsche on the side of the street, next to the Pancake House. She was out of her seat and sitting on his lap, the steering wheel pressing into her back as she returned his kiss.

For the remaining two blocks, they rolled their windows down, because they'd fogged up the windows while making out. She fanned her face with her hand, smiling at Dominic who stuck his head out into the night air.

She laughed herself silly, remembering this moment. No longer was Dominic too serious. He'd joked, he'd laughed, and he'd gone crazy. Spontaneity suited him.

In the parking lot, Dominic paced the outside length of the car. She smothered her laugh, holding her purse over her arm.

"This isn't good for my health." Dominic paused, looked down at the front of his jeans. "Give me another minute."

She couldn't hold her laughter in any longer, and cracked up. He glared, but the skin at the corner of his eyes crinkled.

"This is your fault. You and your smart idea to get me all worked up in the car." He stretched and jogged in place. "My idea of going back to the condominium would solve all my problems right now."

She nodded, laughing. "Big problems."

"Yes." He stalked toward her. "Enormous problems."

"World record breaking kinda huge problems." She leaned into him.

He kissed her. "Now you're being funny."

"Yeah." She pulled him to the bar. "Let's get going, so I can take care of your problem later."

Chapter Nineteen

The party room at Julia's Bar and Grill held every member of the Sharks team, plus all the women who came with their significant other. Dominic rested his hand on the chair beside him and lifted the mug of beer to his mouth. Diana stood a couple yards away, throwing a dart toward the board, after Joel Greene, the Sharks forward, challenged her to a game.

She squealed as the dart hit the board. Dominic smiled. His cheeks ached for how much he found himself grinning around her. She delighted in everything she faced, whether it was learning to skate, dancing, or going toe to toe with the meanest of his women fans. She was fearless and compassionate. An irresistible combination. One that he found himself addicted to and wanting to keep to himself.

He went to bed every night craving to know more about her, to know every part of her, and to know how to put a smile on her face. Then in the morning, he repeated the cycle, hoping this was the day he'd have her completely to himself.

That'd all change tonight. Everything was going smoothly. Life couldn't be so cruel to take this time away from them again.

Tired of always being by himself, he found her company better than he ever thought. She put every one-night stand to shame. He even enjoyed her pushiness and struggle to stay away from him. Hell, he respected her for that alone. She had guts.

His mother would love her. His father would slap him on the back and nod in approval. She'd love visiting Russia, and experiencing a whole new set of firsts for her.

"Dom. Come and see this," she called.

He rose to his feet. She called him Dom. No one but his family ever used the shortened version of his name.

She snaked her arms around his waist and leaned her cheek against his chest as if it was the most natural movement and they'd been doing it for years. He wrapped her in his embrace. "Did you win?"

"No, but I hit the twenty-five spot. That's really good." She tilted her head. "Can I borrow a dollar?"

"Sure." He dug in his back pocket for his wallet.

She stepped back. "I'll pay you back when we get home."

Home. That was twice she'd referred to his condominium as home. He'd never once called it home, but he liked the sound of it.

He gave her the money. "You're not paying me back, don't be ridiculous. It's a dollar."

"Yes, I will." She handed Joel the dollar. "Thanks for the game. You won fair and square."

Joel shook his head and laughed before plucking his win out of her fingers. "You've got a competitive girl there, Chekovsky. Better hold on to her tight, because she's quite the woman."

Dominic waited until Joel walked away, and directed his attention to Diana. "Can we go back to the condominium now?"

She nodded, giving him a secretive grin. "Let me tell everyone goodbye first."

"Really?" He rolled his shoulders. "Can't you talk to them the next time you see them?"

Diana hesitated, and finally ended shaking her head. "No. I'll be quick. I swear."

While she went around to the tables to talk with the others, he went to the front and paid their tab. For the first time, he realized not one woman bothered him tonight. Not the waitress, not the players' girlfriends, and not the hostess. He hadn't even noticed, because he was concentrating on Diana and thinking about what they'd be doing later.

He leaned against the counter. "Hi."

"Hi." The hostess smiled politely, and counted out his change. "Here you go. I hope you enjoyed your evening. Congratulations on the win tonight. From the sounds coming from the room, it was an exciting game."

"Thank you." He remained in front of her, waiting. When she turned away to straighten the menus, he moved along the counter, following her. "What's your name?"

"Melinda," she spoke softly.

She was cute with straight brown hair, almond shaped eyes, and a shy demeanor. He looked at her nametag, because he'd already forgotten her name.

"It's nice to me you, Melinda. I'm Dominic." He flexed his shoulders.

She nodded. "I know. You're part of the team."

Something was wrong. He rubbed his jaw. Maybe he wasn't close enough. He leaned over the counter, bracing his elbows on the glass. He was going to have to kick it up a notch. "What time do you get off work?"

She ducked her chin. "I'm sorry. I don't date the customers."

He straightened in surprise. "Really?"

Diana's laughter behind him caused him to flinch. He turned around, feeling guilty. Yet under the guilt, the confusion of what was happening left him wondering if he'd been hit in the head during the game and was experiencing an out of body experience.

"Did I really catch you asking another woman out, while I'm living with you?" She planted her fists on her hips and tried to appear stern. She failed. There was no mistaking the laughter lighting her eyes.

He hurried over to her, grabbed her hand, and hustled her out of the door. Outside, he stopped. "Did you see that?"

"Yep."

"She blew me off," he said. "Not even a flicker of excitement over talking with me, Dominic Chekovsky."

"She treated you like road dust, baby." She grinned.

"Shit." He let her go of her and shoved both of his hands in his hair, while walking around in a circle. "You did it. You solved all my problems. I can't believe it. The women are ignoring me."

"In less than two weeks too." She shrugged. "You paid for the best, and I am pretty damn good, don't you think?"

He stopped pacing and stared. "Yes. You're brilliant."

Before now, he never gave a thought of the expense he'd paid to have her help him. Maybe because he knew deep down in his soul, asking her to live with him for two weeks was an excuse to get to know her better. Had she pretended her attraction to him was real to get the money?

The thought that the money came first to her left him chilled. "I don't quite know what to say. Thank you doesn't seem to express what I'm feeling right now."

"It's a shock, I know. You might not even like how boring your life could become when you're not running away or hiding from everyone." She dropped her gaze. "You might even wish that you never hired me and want your old world back."

He blew out his cheeks and let the air out slowly. His chest constricted. Everything was happening too fast. He had to slow things down and get a good grasp of what was going on with them. With him. With her.

She'd turned the women off him. He was free. No one would bother him and yet, something wasn't right. He should be more excited. She'd helped him save his career, his happiness. Maybe it'd take time to understand how huge this change was. Right now, all he could think about was Diana and what this meant for her staying with him.

"Let's go home." He held out his hand.

She clasped his fingers and squeezed. "Can I drive?"

"Yeah, you can drive the Porsche," he said.

Right now, she could have whatever he had. He glanced down at her, taking in the wrinkled brow. He wasn't imagining something going on between them. Diana's determination to come to Julia's Bar seemed like a last minute decision. But she'd been hot for him in the car. So why would she need to come out with the guys? Why was she pulling away from him now when they should be celebrating their success?

Chapter Twenty

Dominic's arm hung over Diana's shoulder. She opened the garage door leading into the condominium, while he talked on his cell phone. Inside the kitchen, she motioned to her room. He nodded in acknowledgement, and kept talking to the assistant coach.

She stripped out of Dominic's Sharks sweatshirt, entered her bedroom, and shut the door. Maybe a shower would snap her out of the doldrums that plagued her on the car ride home. She should be happy. Everything worked out perfectly.

Solving all of Dominic's problems before the deadline was what she wanted. Now she could go back to Cottage Grove and purchase the Ferriday house. She turned on the water in the shower, stripped out of the rest of her clothes. But there was a definite funk in the car on the way back to his place.

There was definitely unfinished business between them. She could not go home without experiencing being with Dominic completely. No longer concerned about her place in his life, she wanted all of him. Maybe then she could go back home and not regret how stubborn she'd been with keeping her distance. All because she was afraid of getting hurt. She was going to hurt regardless if they slept together or not.

The warm water steamed the room, and she stepped under the spray. She hung her head, letting the muscles in her neck stretch. They should be celebrating, and she was in here soothing away her sadness.

What started out as getting Dominic to leave her alone and earning money to move on with her life had turned out to be the best time of her life. Not only had Dominic turned into her friend, she genuinely liked him. Their rapport exceeded any physical attraction and that was saying a lot, because more than anything she wanted to be closer than two people could get. She wanted to be a part of every aspect of his life, and if she left without having sex with him, she'd always wonder and regret it the missed opportunity.

She soaped her body, rinsed off, and stepped out of the shower. After wrapping a towel around herself, she squeezed the ends of her hair semi-dry. She wanted to pout or call Shauna and Kate and bitch about how much she hated her life right now.

She never should have taken the job offer. Underneath all the attitude and denial toward Dominic, she knew he had the capability to break her heart from the moment he first asked her out on a date in Cottage Grove. She'd told him as much the other day and yet she'd continued going further with him.

"Hey, Diana?" Dominic rapped on the door. "Can you come back out?"

"Yeah. Give me a second." She searched her room looking for something to wear, and spotted his hockey jersey.

It was a sign.

She dropped her towel.

If there was one thing she was positive about it was that nothing came free. She'd have to go after what she wanted, and the man standing outside her bedroom was everything she dreamed about.

The cool mesh material slid over her naked body. She shivered in anticipation. If the phone rang, she'd throw it across the room. If someone knocked on the door, she'd make it impossible for Dominic to get up to answer it. If his coach demanded he come to practice, she'd...she'd go with him and screw Dominic on the ice while everyone watched.

But she wasn't going to allow it to go that far. Tonight was her night, dammit.

She swung open the door. Dominic raised his gaze. She stepped into his arms and kissed him. There was no more fooling around.

Hot, hard, aggressive, she showed him exactly how she expected their night to end. He slid his hand underneath her curls and cupped her head as he crashed against the wall. She melted as he pressed her lower back tight against him. Heat rolled off his body, warming hers.

"Damn—" he kissed her again "—sweetheart. I want you—" he palmed her ass "—now."

"Yes." She wiggled away from him, and dragged him to his bedroom.

He picked her up and fell on the bed with her in his arms, holding her against him. Touching, kissing, stripping his clothes off, she flailed beside him in her rush. "Hurry."

"I am." He pushed his jeans off his hips and kicked his legs, sending his pants to the floor.

She nibbled her way across his chest, over the taut muscles. Her nails dug into his shoulders. Dominic laughed and as she peered into his face, realizing the egotistical and serious Dominic was gone. He'd learned to smile and laugh during their time together.

She wanted to tell him her thoughts. "Dominic, I—"

"I know. Me too." Once again, his hand went to her hair. He pushed his fingers through the mass, then lowered his head and touched his lips to her mouth.

His body pressed against hers. She felt his lips on her cheek, her neck, and her hand weaved around his ribs, his waist, drawing him closer. She absorbed every hard angle and plane. The muscles in his back flexed beneath her fingertips. His erection pressed against her.

He sucked on her earlobe, the sound of his breath rasped in her ear. Her eyelids drifted shut as need made her melt. Her heart was at stake here. If she went through with having sex with him, she'd belong completely to him. There would be no denying she was falling in love, but what was going on in his mind?

His hands moved in front of her, sliding between the material of the jersey and her bare skin. The warmth of his body seeped into her skin, and her ambiguity disappeared.

His thumbs brushed her nipples and he whispered, "I've wanted you for so long. To be here, touching you."

He skimmed his thumbnail over the hard tip. She gasped. Jolts of pleasure pinged throughout her body. Desire built, expanded, and demanded more. She touched him, hesitatingly at first, then stroking him more confidently.

His breath grew harsh and fast. She squirmed against him, until he guided her on top of him, and he settled below her. "We're going too fast, sweetheart. I need to slow down."

She sucked her bottom lip between her teeth and clamped down. A moan escaped and she wanted to rush and meet him at the finish line before something happened to stop them. "No. We need to hurry."

He spread his hands on her hips. "Shh. Listen."

She blinked, forcing herself to hear past their ragged breaths, past the soft rustle of her knees rubbing against the comforter on his bed, and she found it impossible to sit still when his warm body pressed between her thighs. Beyond them, silence filled the room.

"Nothing is going to stop us." He gazed up into her eyes, his mouth softening.

She shuddered at the huskiness in his voice. Her fists clenched on his chest. Oh, God.

"Condoms," she hissed, throwing her leg off him and jumping from the bed.

"What?" He propped himself on his elbows, watching her.

She raised her hand and pulled a fistful of hair. How could she be so stupid?

"I don't have any condoms. I wasn't planning on having sex with you when I left Cottage Grove." She scrunched her nose. "I can't believe this. All this time, going back and forth, should I or shouldn't I, will he or won't he, and all the craziness with the women and the police, your coach. I don't even have one measly condom."

She paced the room. "Unbelievable. I planned everything. I even have emergency money stashed in my purse in case I'm ever stuck away from home, but did I think of safe sex? No. Why not? Because you're driving me crazy, that's why."

"Diana?"

"I've ruined everything. When I get back to Cottage Grove, I'm going to buy every freakin' box of condoms at Sal's Pharmacy," she said, turning and walking toward the other side of the room.

"Diana?"

"When Kate and Shauna hear about this, I'll never be able to forget about it. They warned me against you. Kate even made me promise to use a condom." She waved her hand in the air. "But did I listen? No."

"Sweetheart?"

"What?" she snapped.

Dominic held a foil package in his hand. "I've got things covered. Or, I will, once you come over here and stop talking to yourself."

Her shoulders sagged in relief. "Pure genius."

She joined him on the bed. His knuckles brushed her cheekbone and he smiled. "Can I make love to you now?"

The air sizzled. The question felt like warm honey dribbled over her skin on a summer day. She took the condom from him and rolled it over his hard length. He ran his palm up the inside of her leg. She couldn't speak at the slow torture of him almost touching, but not quite, in the area that she wanted him to be in.

He nudged her knees apart, lifted her leg, and helped her back on top of him.

Even as they positioned themselves, he never stopped watching her. He cupped her, rubbed her, and her breathing grew shallow and rapid. He slid his finger along her wetness. She gasped and braced herself on his chest.

"Don't move," he whispered.

He shifted his finger forward and rubbed the very spot she needed him to touch. She squeezed her eyes shut. "Oh, Dom…"

"Look at me, sweetheart."

She hadn't expected that he would take his time, to romance her with words, or to see her own excitement reflected back to her in his eyes. His callused finger slid inside of her. He understood, and he continued pleasuring her, until she shattered into a million pieces.

He stroked her thighs, letting her recover. She blinked away the moisture gathering in her vision. "Dom," she murmured. "That was, oh God, that was freaking wonderful."

"I know." He rolled her over, until he was on top of her, settled between her legs. "But I'm not done with you yet."

She saw the exact moment the ice melted from his eyes and he succumbed to what was happening between them. She reached between their bodies, placed him inside her, and hooked her legs around the back of his thighs.

He began moving slowly. She could feel the tension coiled in his shoulders. Inch by inch, he plunged inside until they were fully connected. He hissed. She cupped his face, and arched her back.

She reveled in his shudder, in the fact that she brought a man his size, his strength, his determination to a level that he trembled in her arms. She felt delirious.

"You feel so good." He moved back and forth, sliding, caressing her from the inside out.

She gave a throaty moan as his thrust sped up. His arms shook in the effort it took to restrain himself. She raised her hips, meeting him halfway as her body rejuvenated below him. She needed more. He deserved more. She locked her ankles behind his back, wrapped her arms around his neck.

Her body tensed, strained, reached. He drove home, and as he fully possessed her, she gazed up into his eyes. The depth of her love for him brought her to a crazy finish. She clutched him as waves of pleasure coursed through her body, and he shuddered his release.

He went down to his elbows, bracing his weight off her, but staying inside of her. She swallowed. Hard.

Emotional and spent, she allowed him to roll her to her side, curling her against him as he pulled the cover over them both. She laid her head against his bare chest. His heart raced against her ear. Only then did she squeeze her eyes closed. *I will not cry. I will not cry.*

Chapter Twenty-One

Diana lost track of how many times Dominic made love to her in the last three days. She would've thought she'd have him out of her system or the newness would wear off. She peered around the corner of the bedroom door at Dominic lounging on the bed with the newspaper. The opposite was true.

She couldn't get enough of the big guy.

Playful, serious, entranced, dedicated, athletic. He'd shown her multiple sides of himself in bed and out. Throughout the best thirteen days of her life, there was one thing she'd been dying to do and so far, she hadn't been brave enough to ask him.

Until now.

She sauntered into the room wearing another one of his jerseys after taking a quick shower. "Hey."

The newspaper in front of him lowered. He gazed at her intently, his mouth softening as he set aside the sports section. "Hey you."

She stood at the side of the bed, her hands behind her back, and looked everywhere but at him. Although she watched him in her peripheral vision, she'd chicken out if she had to face him.

When she'd finally found what she was looking for in the kitchen on top of the refrigerator after making coffee for them both, she'd thought of nothing else than asking him for one huge favor. Now that she was standing in front of him, nervousness hit her.

He'd think she was silly asking him to do this for her. She lifted her bare foot and crossed her legs. She should turn and go back out. He'd never know what was going through her mind.

"What do you have behind your back, sweetcheeks?" he asked.

Oh, God. She bit down on her lip. It was now or never, and she did not want to go home knowing she balked, because she was too worried about him laughing at her.

"Um, I was wondering…" She sat on the edge of the bed, her back away from him, and her hands still hidden from his view. "You know when we first met?"

"Yes. At the field in Cottage Grove." He leaned over, spanned her waist with his hands, picked her up, and plopped her down on his stomach. "You ignored me."

"Yeah, well, um." She grimaced, settling down on top of him. "I can be a snob."

"No…" He chuckled. "You?"

She bounced on him and glared. "You're not supposed to agree."

"You were adorable. Sexy. Unforgettable," he murmured.

His gaze warmed and his hands went to her thighs, underneath the material of her shirt. Quicker than she could brace herself, he'd moved her until she sat on his erection. She warmed. "Oh, boy," she whispered. "Okay. This is good."

"Very good." He continued touching her, caressing her skin, and looking at her with those fabulous blue eyes of his that could go from ice to innocence in one blink.

If she didn't ask him now, she never would, and she had to see him do it one more time before she went back to Cottage Grove. She thrust his sunglasses in front of her and smiled on a shrug. "Do you think you could wear these?"

His brows rose. "Now?"

She nodded. "Please?"

He took his black sunglasses from her and glanced at her again. "We're in the house."

"Yeah." She braced her hands on his chest and leaned forward, liking the way he felt between her legs. Even though they were having a conversation, she found sitting on his hardness a little distracting and too enjoyable. "You're hot. That first time I saw you, you were wearing them. You had your thugs behind you and they were wearing sunglasses too. I became overwhelmed, because I'd never met someone so famous they came with a security team. But what I remembered, and I can't seem to forget, was how damn sexy and hot you looked standing there with your arms crossed, your shades on…and despite a gazillion women fluttering around you…you only looked at me. Even with your sunglasses on, I could tell, you only had eyes on me. From that day on, I knew you were my weakness. I fought. I argued. I was a royal bitch," she ended on a whisper. "Because deep down, I wanted you."

She hadn't planned on spilling her guts to him or confessing to how much he'd turned her on from the first minute they met.

For several seconds Dominic didn't say anything. She started to get off him, when he took the sunglasses, put them on, and flipped her over onto her back. Her body came alive. Excitement, Lust. Love. Hope. Anticipation. All her emotions tangled together.

"Dom…"

He remained silent and all she could concentrate on was the feel of his hard body settled between her legs. Her thin mesh jersey top she borrowed from him was no barrier to the heat that rolled off him. Her nipples hardened and ached. She dragged in a deep breath, and trailed her hands up his arm, over his shoulders.

His eyes were hidden behind the sunglasses, his lips parted. "You, Diana Spenner, are the only woman who I have ever wanted to look at."

Oh, geez. She liked that. A lot.

There was no way she could hide her reaction to his confession, not from a man who knew every type of woman and enjoyed them his whole life. And she was his favorite. The warmth she was experiencing coiled deep inside of her.

She was practically panting as she reached between them and pulled his boxers out of the way. "Condom?"

He stretched to the side, never leaving his position between her thighs, and grabbed another condom off the nightstand. With ease, he ripped open the foil, covered himself, and brought his attention to her. Her lashes fluttered shut and she held herself still, barely breathing.

"Open your eyes," he whispered, his words thick with control.

Diana wasn't sure if she could look at him, but then his mouth was crushing hers and everything about the moment became him. The way he touched her. The feel of his lips pressing down, eliciting a response from her—one she couldn't deny. Her emotions tumbled out in a raw, soul-burning phenomenon. She wanted him now. Hard and fast. Her and him.

His tongue, moist and demanding, parried with hers. There was an urgent possessiveness in the way he kissed her. Every kiss she'd ever experienced in the past, every boyfriend she'd ever dated, every fantasy she'd created in her head burned away with the memories Dominic created for her. From right now, there was only him.

One hand came off the bed and he stroked her heat with his finger, opening her, and guiding himself in. He slowly plunged into her wetness, holding himself there with more control than she was feeling herself. She ached for him.

Dominic withdrew, then thrust again, and the whole time he stared down at her. She didn't have to see his eyes behind the sunglasses, because she knew he only looked at her.

She locked her legs around his hips and hooked her arms around his neck. Dominic came down to his elbows, continually riding her body. She arched up to kiss him. To her surprise, Dominic kissed her back, but took total control.

He was gentle, and so sweet she thought all her dreams were coming true. She moaned. Her body spiraled higher. Oh, God.

His hands, his thighs, his hips claimed her. But his mouth showed her what he wasn't saying in words. Staked to the bed, consumed by everything Dominic, Diana cried out his name in the most wonderful, soulful release. He'd gone still, his breathing ragged a millisecond before he groaned, burying his head in her neck.

It was in that quiet moment, Diana saw something so beautiful, so potent, and so scary, she knew without a doubt what she must do. Her stomach soured at the thought. She'd convinced herself she could return to Cottage Grove with no regrets.

It was too late.

She loved Dominic with every breath in her body. He'd opened her eyes, showed her a side of him she would never have seen— that no other person had seen. If he hadn't stalked her and not given up, her life would be poorer.

She squeezed her eyes closed. Now she was sitting on a half million dollars, in love with a professional hockey player who couldn't be in her life, and her dream of owning the Ferriday house were coming true. She should be happy. Her arms tightened around Dominic. All she could think about was how little time they had left together.

Chapter Twenty-Two

In the hectic rush of Dominic getting ready for the Sharks versus Red Wings game, Diana carried her luggage out to the living room. She'd already washed the bedding, remade the bed, cleaned the bathroom, and stolen his jersey. There was nothing left to do.

Dominic would take her to the airport on his way to the game. If she stopped for too long, thought too much about the moment, she'd start crying. She'd never voiced what she really wanted.

He never asked her to stay, and deep in her heart, she knew her life was back in Cottage Grove. Once she arrived at the hotel, she'd let herself have a good cry for losing a man who'd stolen her heart. Then she'd walk to the real estate office and slap down the money for the Ferriday house to get over how hard it was going to be to find the strength to walk away from someone like Dominic.

Dominic's keys jingled. She turned and winced. The serious Dominic was back. His eyes colder than ice stared back at her.

"Do you want to drive?" He tilted his head to the side.

She picked one of the bags off the floor. "No, you can."

He ran his tongue over his teeth, his jaw twitching. "I'll get the rest of the bags and put them in the trunk."

"Thanks." She followed him into the garage.

On the road, she stared at his hand on the gearshift. The white scars over his knuckles from all the rough play on the rink, the broad width of years of building his muscles, and the callouses from hours of work and dedication for a sport he loved would stay engraved in her head for the rest of time. Yet all she could conjure at the moment was the soft touch of his fingers against her skin. She sighed.

"You okay?" He reached over and squeezed her hand.

She nodded. "Yeah. I just…"

"What?"

"I'm happy we became friends, Dom." She smiled. "Thank you for asking me to help you. I'll never forget you or the last two weeks."

He glanced out the side window. "Me, neither, sweetcheeks."

Geez. Sweetcheeks. She'd even miss him calling her fat when he really didn't mean she was *fat*.

At the small runway for private aircrafts, Dominic handed her items over to the co-pilot. She stood alongside the plane, not ready to go. There were so many things she hadn't told him, so many things they hadn't done. Most of all, she waited for him to change her mind about leaving. All she needed was him asking her to stay.

Dominic walked over to her. She held her breath. This was it.

He reached into his pocket, removed his wallet, and withdrew a check. "Here you go. If you have any problems cashing it, let me know."

She stared at the zeroes until they all blurred together and were unrecognizable. She forced a laugh. "Don't forget, my dad's a banker, remember?"

"Right." He looked off into the distance.

"I won't forget about naming one of the rooms after the great hockey player Dominic Chekovsky either. It'll be the best room at the bed and breakfast." She laughed softly to keep from crying. "Any time you want to stay at the B and B, I won't even charge you."

His mouth hardened. She frowned.

"Dom?" She stepped in front of him and waited for him to look at her.

He'd closed himself off. She wanted to tell him to keep playing hockey in his socks, to dance and forget about time, and to drive with the top down on the Porsche with the radio cranked full blast. Yet she was afraid he'd do that with some other woman, and she couldn't find the strength to think about what comes next for him.

"I better get on the plane." She rose onto her tiptoes and kissed him soft and long. The warmth that always came filled her chest and she trembled. Forcing herself to go before she changed her mind, she stepped back. "I'll see you in Cottage Grove some time, right?"

He inhaled deeply. "Maybe."

"Goodbye, Dom." She smiled sadly.

"Have a safe flight, sweetcheeks," he whispered.

She turned away before he saw her tears. The co-pilot helped her into the charter plane and she sat down, buckling the harness. When the plane rolled forward, she turned to the window.

Dominic stood watching the plane, his hands shoved deep in his pockets. She put her fingers on the glass. He dropped his chin to his chest, turned, and walked away from her.

• • •

Four hours later, Dominic sat in the penalty box after letting his anger continue to fester over letting Diana walk away. He itched to get back in the game after a five-minute penalty. There were three minutes to go in the last half of the game, and he wanted back in. More than anything he wanted Craig Brown, and he wanted to make him hurt.

Hurt the way he'd hurt Diana. It was as if she couldn't wait to leave him, and that confused him. They'd grown closer during their time together.

Last night, he thought he'd won the lottery. He'd lain there in her embrace, his hips resting between her thighs, her arms around his neck, and their breath mingling. For the first time, he felt at home. After all these years of coping with his schedule, his life, his career, and being away from his home country, he'd reveled in knowing he was right where he wanted to be for the rest of his life.

Nothing, not his parents, hockey, his team, his community brought him the peace and contentment that Diana gave him. Every time she looked at him, he filled with energy. He wanted to do better, go bigger, and be a man she could be proud to walk beside. He loved teasing her, because he noticed the way she drew closer until her body softened against him. His chest tightened. He wanted to protect her and make sure she'd never leave him.

He hit his hockey stick against the wall holding him back. Anger built inside of him. He already missed her.

She'd walked out of his life, and he let her go like a fool. The last smile she gave him said everything. He'd hurt her. He'd failed. He'd lost her.

Maybe he was foolish to believe they could work something out between them. Was it even fair of him to ask her to tie herself to life with a hockey player who had to put the team first and spend his days on the rink?

All he had to do was get through this game, and then he could deal with what happened today. He ground his teeth together and concentrated on the penalty clock. All he needed was time to get his head in the right spot, the game behind him, and then he'd figure out his next move.

He'd fucked up.

Useless to stop Diana from walking away from him, he deserved all the torment he was under. Nothing was the same without her by his side. He had no idea what any woman wanted from him, especially Diana.

She'd accused him of wanting her for sex, and he'd let her walk away as if all they had was a good time and it was over. He'd lived up to her original opinion of him. *Shit.*

The buzzer went off and the door swung open. He raced out across the ice, picking up the pass from the forward, and skated full speed ahead. Brown zeroed in on him from the side, he passed the puck off, cut across the blue line, and came out behind his opponent. He trailed the edge of his stick along the ice, waiting.

The opening came the same time Brown glanced behind him. He captured the puck. Left, right, left, raised his stick, and Brown crushed him against the board. He bounced back, punching the other player in the face. His head snapped to his shoulder, and he continued to wail.

The referee forged between them. Bradley skated in and pushed him away from Brown. He ripped off his gloves, his helmet, and threw them across the ice.

"Check it, man." Bradley got in his face. "Coach is going to have your ass. That's three penalties in one game."

"Go to hell." He pushed himself away and slid back in the penalty box.

He looked at the scoreboard. Hell. Game over. The Sharks won, but he still ran strong and hot. He studied the stands, going straight to Diana's spot in the team's private area. The seat next to Stephanie's was empty.

Nobody paid him any attention. The women cheered for the team, not the man in the penalty box. He leaned back and hit the bench. He should've asked Diana to stay.

The whole morning he could tell she had something to say, and then he'd catch her walking away. He'd wanted to talk to her. She had one more day of vacation left. They could've spent it together. Maybe even taken the time to visit the local beach or go sightseeing. He hadn't shown her everything he promised.

The buzzer rang. He left the box, skated toward the huddle of players, and went through the after game motions. His heart wasn't in the game today.

He avoided Coach and hit the showers. All invitations to join the players at Julia's Bar and Grill bounced off him, and he shrugged his way out of the locker room when his teammates tried to talk with him. He had nothing to say.

The fans gathered at the back door of the arena. He ignored the cheers and walked straight to his car. Truly alone and unbothered, he drove to the condominium.

The inside of the Porsche smelled of jasmine. He cranked the radio. The Top Forty station blared. Not wanting to listen to Diana's favorite music, he switched the station and let DDT fill the car.

With another practice tomorrow and a game after that, he couldn't leave. He ignored the road leading to the condominium, and kept driving. Not ready to go back to an empty house, he hit the highway.

Diana had woven herself into his life, and nothing remained the same. Not hockey, not his social life, and not his bed. He pushed the accelerator down, and wished she were here to laugh as he speeded along. She delighted in the smallest things, and made him enjoy every second with her.

Red and blue lights flashed in his rearview mirror. He slowed down and turned on his blinker. *Shit.*

Coach would not be happy over him getting a ticket and making the news. He shut off the engine and let his hands fall in his lap. He was falling apart.

Chapter Twenty-Three

The Quayside Lounge buzzed with the usual Friday night crowd. Diana sat next to the window in the back, across from Kate, Shauna, and a visiting Crista for their Girls' Night Out. Her mood fought with the upbeat music playing, and the Cosmo she'd nursed the last hour only marginally made the night tolerable.

"Should we join the guys in the game room?" Kate took a compact mirror out of her purse and applied lipstick. "Maybe some testosterone will lighten the mood."

"Shh." Shauna elbowed Kate. "We're doing fine out here. This is fun. I don't want to watch no stupid game on television with the guys."

The game room slash sports bar of the lounge was playing the San Jose Sharks game, no doubt. Diana shook her head. "Go ahead. I'm going to make it an early night."

"Diana..." Shauna leaned against the table. "Tell us what happened. You left town without telling any of us how you felt about going off with Dominic, and you've hid in your room at the hotel since you got back. We're worried about you. I thought you and Dominic were getting together, or at least into each other."

"There's nothing to say." She finished the rest of her drink. "I had a job, and now it's time to get back to my normal life."

Crista wadded her napkin. "I don't even know what you guys are talking about. It seems like I miss all the gossip when I'm gone." She crossed her arms. "Which stops now, because I'm supposed to be your friend. But if it has to do with Dominic, I can guess what happened. Diana fell for Dominic's seductive ways. It happens every single time. I don't know how many times I've seen women walk away from him with a broken heart. It's a crime."

"Why haven't you ever ended up with him?" Diana sat up straighter. "I mean, you've known Dominic longer than I have."

"I tried...sorta. Well, at least as much as Dominic allowed someone to get close to him emotionally. We hung out." Crista shrugged. "We didn't have sex, if you're curious, but I made a fool of myself over him like all the other women. Dominic pretty much ignored me. Now I just make sure I'm never alone with him, because I don't want to embarrass myself. It helps that when I do see him, I'm usually in training and all I have on my mind is the race. End of history."

"Diana doesn't do anything stupid. She's the most secure, rational, organized person I know." Shauna waved her hand at the waitress, waited for her to approach, and then ordered another round of drinks. "You can't go to the hotel until we get the whole story about what happened between your phone calls to me, and arriving in Cottage Grove looking like you broke the heel on a pair of Jimmy Choos."

"Let's change the subject," she said. "Isn't Grayson looking for you?"

"Probably, but we have a bet on who can go without sex the longest again. It's been twenty-four hours and if I'm around him after I have a drink, I'll lose.

"My God, that's the stupidest competition I've ever heard of you two doing. I'd never do such a thing with Jackson. I'd be a bitch. A whole day? Give it up." Kate zipped her purse, laughing. "I swear, you two make me sick. You can't keep your hands off each other."

"Why would you bet on that?" Diana asked.

Shauna rolled her eyes. "I read this article about how the longer between sexual activities you go, the more powerful it is when you finally do have sex. I want to find out if there's any truth to the

experiment. So far, we keep starting over because we screw up...
literally."

Diana waited until the drinks arrived and then appeased her
curiosity. "What did Grayson bet you? There has to be more to
the story."

"There is, and since I don't keep secrets like you, I'll share with
everyone. Maybe you'll learn from my example." Shauna grinned
and softened her lecture toward Diana with a blown kiss. "If I
lose, I have to go to Cancun with him. You girls know me better
than that, right? Cancun was the prize the whole time. I just didn't
let him know it was my idea. He'll think he won, and I'll get my
tan on somewhere away from the press and his fans."

"Life of the rich and famous," Diana muttered.

"Hey!" All three of her friends shouted.

She held up her hands, and smiled for the first time since
sitting down at the table. "Sorry. I forget that I'm the only one in
our group who lives for payday."

"What about the money you earned from—" Kate clapped her
hand over her mouth and groaned. "I'm so, so sorry. Me and my
big mouth."

"It's okay." Diana leaned her head over on Kate's shoulder. "My
secret won't be a secret after tomorrow."

"What's going on?" Crista scooted her chair closer to the table.
"I might not get to visit with you all very often, but I care about
you and want to know what is happening in your lives."

How did she explain that she'd pimped herself out to Dominic
for the sole purpose of buying her own bed and breakfast? No
matter what she said, she came away sounding selfish.

"I stayed with Dominic to help him with a problem. You all
know how all the women act around him. So I pretended to be his
girlfriend and chased them all away. In return he paid me...a lot
of money," she whispered. "I'm not proud of the fact, but it was an
honest job offer and he was satisfied with how I worked for him.

By the time my two weeks were over, none of the women paid any attention to him."

Her whole story was an understatement. So much more happened, but she wasn't ready to share. The wound of losing him fresh in her mind, she still hurt. Even worse, not being around him all the time pained her, when he probably slid right back into his life of hockey with no problems.

Of course, by now, everyone knew she'd left him and he probably had a whole horde of women stalking him. Neither one of them thought about what would happen after she left and he no longer had her to use as his pretend girlfriend any longer.

The thought of him going out tonight after the game to celebrate and having women hang on him caused her stomach to ache. He probably wasn't even thinking about her, because someone else occupied his mind.

Her phone on her lap rang. She jumped. "Excuse me."

She walked away from the table and peered at the screen, frowning. *How did she get my number?*

She walked down the hallway to the bathrooms where she could hear better. "Stephanie?"

"Oh, good, you answered."

"What's wrong?" she asked.

"Dominic. Coach fined him twenty two thousand for excess penalties tonight at the game."

She frowned. "What? He never gets more than two penalties a game. What happened?"

"He's skating hot. Nobody can talk to him without him blowing up and starting fights." Stephanie sighed. "That's not the worst of it though."

"I can't believe this…" She rubbed her forehead. "What else?"

"Bradley overheard Coach threatening to put him on the trading list…"

"Oh, no." She bowed her head. "Dominic doesn't want to go somewhere else. He loves the Sharks."

"According to Bradley, Dominic told Coach to let him know what he decides on his future. When Coach yelled at him, Dominic walked out of the meeting. Bradley tried to stop him, but Dominic said he'd rather go back to Russia than play where he's not wanted."

Diana's chest tightened. "Hockey's his life. He wouldn't walk away."

"You haven't seen him lately, Diana. He's broken since you've left. His game is off, he's pulled away from his teammates, and he's basically giving the coach the finger when he shows up at practice," Stephanie said.

"What are you saying?" she whispered.

"Everyone thinks he's falling apart because you left him." Stephanie paused. "You can fix everything. Talk to him and tell him he's ruining his career. He'll listen to you, I know he will."

"I didn't—" She clamped her lips closed.

"Call him. Please?"

"I-I can't." She swallowed over the lump in her throat. "Steph… we were never together, for real."

Stephanie remained silent. She closed her eyes for a moment to stop the tears from coming. "Whatever's going through Dominic's head, it has nothing to do with me. Honest. He let me go. We had an agreement, and my time there ended. We went our separate ways as friends."

Or, she'd thought they had. Her head pounded. Something was going on, because Dominic would never give up hockey without a fight.

"I thought better of you, and I really liked you." Stephanie cleared her throat. "I gave it my best shot. I thought you'd care, but it's obvious you don't. All the Sharks were depending on me to find a way to help Dominic, and…never mind. You weren't a real fan anyway. All you did was pretend to love Dominic and hurt him."

"Steph. Don't say that. I do care about him, and you, the team," she said.

"I better go. I need to fill the guys in and let them know I failed to get you to help. Goodbye."

The phone clicked in her ear. Diana dropped her arm. Dominic had let her walk away. It was just a coincidence that he was having trouble on the ice. He'd pull through. Wouldn't he?

Or she could call him. She peered down at the screen of her cell. No. It was over between them. He didn't want her, because he let her walk away. It wasn't her job anymore to interfere in his life. He could handle whatever trouble he got himself into by himself.

She headed down the hallway, caught a glimpse of Grayson and Kate's boyfriend Jackson at the sports bar, and stopped. The television played the Sharks versus the Rangers pre-recorded game on the big screen television above the bar. Without making a conscious decision, she walked inside and claimed a spot at the end of the bar. She'd see for herself what kind of trouble Dominic caused on the rink.

At first, she couldn't spot him on the rink, and then he skated out of the penalty box. She gripped onto the edge of the counter, leaning forward. The graceful flow of the moves she was used to seeing when he was out on the ice were jerky, hurried, and tense.

"Hey, Diana…" Grayson touched her arm.

She glanced between him and the flat screen television. "Hi."

"Why don't I walk you back to the women? You don't need to watch the game. As hockey goes, it's the same old thing." He cupped her elbow.

She jerked away. "No. I want to watch."

"Hon." Grayson sighed. "I won't lie to you. Dominic's off his game. It's not pretty."

She flinched as on the television screen, Dominic landed against the wall in a bone-jarring hit. "Have you talked to him?"

"Yeah. I called him. He's home. The game's recorded."

"Is he okay? I mean, does he sound fine?" She pressed her hand against her stomach, not taking her eyes off the screen. "I don't understand what he's doing. He's back in the penalty box. Dominic never gets a temper on the ice."

"He says he's fine. I couldn't get him to talk about the game. He said he's making everything right, though," Grayson said. "You have to understand the life of a professional athlete. A lot goes on behind the scenes, and he'll survive. He loves the sport."

She shoved her hand into her purse and extracted her phone. "I've got to call him. Stephanie was right. Something huge is wrong with Dominic."

"Why don't you give him some time?" Grayson motioned over her head. "Shauna's coming in. Talk to her."

"I don't want to talk to anyone but Dominic." She cussed and pulled the cell away from her ear to look at the screen. "He's not answering. Why wouldn't he answer the phone if he told you he was home?"

"He's okay—"

Voicemail clicked on. "Dom. It's Diana. Call me…please. It doesn't matter when, but soon. I need to talk with you." She disconnected the call and stood. "I have to get out of here."

Shauna stepped in front of her. "Come back and have another drink first. You should hang with your friends."

She shook her head. "I want to go to the hotel and see if Dominic called and left a message there. Maybe he forgot my cell number."

"I'll walk with you." Shauna slipped her arm under Diana's elbow and nodded at Grayson. "Pick me up in an hour at the hotel, okay?"

"Yeah, babe." Grayson kissed Shauna's cheek.

Diana walked back to the hotel with Shauna. Deep inside her head, she didn't worry about not talking. Shauna gave her room to think.

Whatever was going on with Dominic wasn't about his female fans bothering him again. Over the television, she would've heard the cheering when he skated out on the ice. Instead, the Sharks' support sounded normal. Something else was going on, and the thought that he'd go back to Russia scared her.

Chapter Twenty-Four

Dominic drove the Porsche out of the garage and hit the remote button, locking the condominium. He had three days off and orders from Coach to get his head back into playing hockey before he'd be allowed to play in the next scheduled game against the Rangers.

In the past twenty-four hours, Dominic had completely turned his life around. Never one to put stock in money, except as a means to help support his family back in Russia, he was glad for the added pull a pouch full of money could buy him.

Once he'd gotten down to business and set a plan in his personal life, he sucked it up and met with his coach in a three-hour meeting. He explained what happened the other night at the game and promised on his home country of Russia it wouldn't happen again. He turned onto the main road. Luckily, Coach gave him another shot.

Twenty minutes later, he parked the car and climbed into the private charter plane. He sat in the rear seat of the Cessna, heading north to Cottage Grove. He owed Grayson a beer.

Most importantly, he wanted to talk with Diana.

She'd left three messages. His phone rang. He looked at the screen and grinned. Make that four.

What he had to say was too important to talk about over the phone. He ignored the ringtone and let the call go to voicemail. She deserved more than a thank you over the cell.

Diana stole from him. Without even telling him, she took something of his without asking first, and he wanted it back. He tapped his thumb against his thigh. There was no other explanation for how his jersey came up missing. She must've taken it.

"We'll be landing in five minutes," said the pilot.

He buckled his seatbelt and peered out over the wing. He couldn't wait to see Diana. She'd brought normalcy and enjoyment back into his life. He inhaled deeply, trying to calm his racing heart. He missed her slow smile and quick laugh. She'd become such a major part of his life in such a short time—without her, he realized, a part of himself was missing.

Independence and success often meant a lonely life. For him it was true, especially when people pushed their way into his life. Not Diana. She'd dragged her feet and put up a good fight, but once she'd made up her mind, she gave her all to him. Fierce and determined, she showed him her soft, vulnerable side and hooked him.

The plane came to a stop. He followed the pilot out the door, spotted Grayson leaning against his car, and headed in that direction.

Always the calm and cool athlete, Grayson stood stoically out on the runway. "Right on time."

"Everything go okay?" Dominic threw his bag into the truck. "You didn't run into any troubles getting everything done for me, did you?"

Grayson slapped him on the shoulder. "Nope, everything went smoothly. I set everything up, just like you asked. But you left a hell of a mess. Shauna tried to do damage control, but you even have her confused."

"You didn't mention anything to Shauna, did you?" he asked.

Grayson shook his head. "I've kept myself busy at the tennis center and tried to stay away from her and the girls. You know I can't keep anything secret around Shauna...and she is asking me what is going on, but lucky for us, she went to Kate instead.

Last I heard they were going to converge at the hotel and plot an intervention or burn voodoo dolls in replicas of men they know."

He climbed into the car and grinned. "That'll keep Diana busy. There's no way she'll find out I'm here and what I'm doing."

"I don't know. Those girls have their way of finding out everything that happens in Cottage Grove. It's damn scary how that happens." Grayson drove off the field toward Cottage Grove. "Right now, I'm sure they're planning a way to hang us by the balls."

"No…"

Grayson shook his head. "Yes."

"Shit." He gazed out the window. "Would you have done what I did?"

"Yeah." Grayson shrugged. "But, you're going to have a helluva time making it up to her. If Diana is anything like Shauna, you'll enjoy getting on her good side."

He closed his eyes and groaned. If he would've talked to Diana first, she would've told him no. Stingy and proud, she'd never listen to reason. Hopefully, she'd realize why he came to Cottage Grove and forgive him.

• • •

Diana walked out of the credit union and leaned against the brick wall. Her hands perspired, and she closed her eyes against the nausea making her dizzy. After wrestling with her blankets all night, she'd decided to do the one thing she'd sworn never to do.

She got a loan, and not from her father.

Just thinking about all the papers she signed moments ago, only to receive pre-approval to purchase the Ferriday house, left her wondering if she'd survive writing her name on the dotted line when she offered to buy the house and it was officially hers. She swung her purse over her shoulder and pushed off the wall. Only thing left to do is walk across the street to the real estate office and write up an official offer.

Dominic's check weighed heavier on her mind than in her purse. She'd finally figured out last night the reason she put off running to the realtor the moment the plane landed was because of how she felt about being paid to fall in love with him.

She couldn't use his money. She'd hate herself for the rest of her life.

Their time together meant more than a half a million dollars, and if she cashed the check, she'd forever know how much she lost. She held up her hand to stop traffic and crossed the street. Despite her broken heart, she couldn't take money he'd normally send to his parents. The image of him as a little boy playing sock hockey in the basement with his parents cheering him on deserved the money more than her.

When all was said and done, she'd given him a couple of weeks of privacy in his crazy life but in the long run, he'd forget about her. She stepped onto the curb. Giving the money back would allow her to go on with her life; she could move on to running her own bed and breakfast, and Dominic would play hockey and enjoy his freedom to choose the right girl for him.

"Diana?" Her mom's voice reached her.

She turned in surprise. "Hi, Mom."

Tara Spenner, fifty-eight years old, trim, and exceedingly professional appearing in her black blazer and pencil skirt, hurried toward Diana. Diana put the envelope of papers she'd received from the bank behind her back out of guilt. Her mom was going to flip when she found out she'd used all her savings as a down payment.

"Sweetheart." Mom kissed her cheek. "You haven't called or stopped by the bank since you arrived back in town. Your dad and I are worried about you. You're not acting normal, going off with a man we don't even know. What has gotten into you lately?"

She laughed self-consciously. "It was a little vacation, Mom. That's all. I called and left a message, remember?"

"Yes, but a man, Diana? We had no idea you were seeing anyone." Her mom's voice softened. "Are you okay?"

"I'm fine." She smiled. "Better than fine, really. I-I'm buying a house."

"What?" Mom pulled back. "But with your wages at the hotel, you aren't scheduled to have enough money to afford your own house until you're twenty-eight years old. Your dad has your portfolio at the bank, why don't you find time to go sit down with him and he can help you figure out how to put more money into an IRA. Besides, what about the hotel? It's free rent as long as you're working there, and a great place for someone young and pretty to meet—"

"Yes, but I want to own a bed and breakfast, Mom." She paused and looked at the door of the real estate office. "I'm not satisfied working for someone else. I need to grow and learn. I love making others happy, giving them the best accommodations and helping them enjoy their stay in Cottage Grove. I want that satisfaction of supplying a need for the town. It's a good business decision. Cottage Grove doesn't have a bed and breakfast, just the hotel."

"I don't think your planning this right. You've got yourself mixed up with some man who's giving you all these ideas. It's ridiculous. When your father hears—"

"No, Mom. My decision has nothing to do with a man. If I screw up then I'll be the one to pay the price. Not you. Not Dad. Me." She sighed. "I have an appointment, and if I don't go, I'll be late getting back to work. I'm on my lunch hour, so I must hurry."

"Diana?"

"I can't talk right now. I'll call you tonight, okay?" She opened the door, and rushed in the building without waiting for a reply.

If she gave herself two minutes to discuss her plans with her parents, she'd chicken out. Paying on a loan for the next thirty years went against everything she believed in when it came to investing her money. Financial security was the one thing she could count on to keep her safe, happy, and content.

"Diana." Sue Patrick walked out of her office. "Come on back to my office, and we can sit down."

"Thank you." She followed the forty-year-old woman and mother of two girls, and took the seat across from the desk. "I'm glad you were able to see me on such short notice."

"My pleasure." Sue clasped her hands together on the desk. "What can I help you with today?"

She fingered the edge of the manila envelope. "You know I've been interested in the real estate market lately, and you've been so nice to send me all the listings when I've asked for them." She smiled. "I've made a decision. I'd like to make an offer for the Ferriday house on Baltimore Street."

Anxiety whooshed out of her with the words, and she laughed in relief. She'd wanted to make that announcement for the last three years, ever since she'd returned from college. Nothing could stop her now. She'd held strong against her mother, worked her ass off at the hotel, and the paperwork was only a formality.

"Oh, no. I'm afraid I have bad news for you." Sue leaned back in her chair. "I'm sorry, Diana, but the Ferriday house went off the market early this morning."

"What?" Not possible. That was her house.

"A cash buyer approached me last night, offered full price, and the lawyer in charge of the estate accepted early this morning," Sue said.

Gone? Diana stared at the desk. What about her bed and breakfast? The renovations? Her future?

"I would be more than glad to help you search for another house." Sue clicked the mouse and brought up a different screen on the computer. "We have an older, one story house on Oak Street, across from the middle grade school. The house has all the original woodwork and is in great shape for the age. The new listing came on the market last week."

"No. Um, no, thank you." She stood.

"I'm sorry again, Diana." Sue's bottom lip came out in understanding. "Please call me if there is anything I can do for you in the future."

She nodded, numb and heartbroken. In a daze, she walked outside. How could someone buy the house after all these years? It'd been on the market since she returned from college. And now, someone bought it and probably wanted to knock it down and build something new. She walked along the sidewalk. Her dream was over. There were no other houses of that caliber in Cottage Grove that would fit her ideal of a historical bed and breakfast.

"Diana." Her dad's baritone voice broke through her thoughts. She raised her gaze off the sidewalk, spotted Jerry Spenner, and ran into his arms. "Oh, Dad, someone bought the house."

"Shh." He patted her back. "Your mom told me what you were doing."

She sniffed. "I know you don't approve, but I wanted that house. It's all I've thought about for the last three years."

"I know," he said.

She pulled back. His freshly shaved face, his gleaming glasses, and gray hair didn't distract her from the understanding smile he aimed at her. "How?"

"Cottage Grove is a small town, honey." He swiped her cheek with his finger. "I own the main bank, and I also know you weren't putting your wages in my bank. It wasn't hard to figure out you had other plans. Besides, I saw the list you'd made on your table last time I visited you. It wasn't hard to put all the information together and guess what you were up to."

"You're not disappointed?"

He chuckled. "No, I'm proud, so very proud of you. You're young, single, and the most headstrong person in our family. If anyone could make a success of a bed and breakfast in Cottage Grove, you could've with no problems."

"But you and Mom…"

"We were young once too. We struggled and fought, and you've only seen the benefits of what took years and years to accomplish. You might not believe it, but there was a time we were wild and lived on our last dollar, because we thought traveling to Portland, Oregon to a concert or driving cross country with a group of our friends to go skiing was more important than whether we had macaroni for dinner or steak."

Shocked and intrigued by the image of her careless parents, she shook her head and sighed. "I don't know what I'm going to do now."

"You pick yourself up, go back to work at the hotel, and keep saving so the next time an opportunity knocks at your door, you'll be ready." He lifted her chin. "Then if you need anything, you come to me. I'll help you."

She kissed his cheek. "Thanks, Dad."

"Now, tell me about this man you snuck away to stay with." Her dad frowned. "A professional athlete? That's quite a change of lifestyle from what you're used to here."

She glanced away. "It's nothing. I just helped a friend of a friend."

She couldn't think about what a mess her life was at this moment. She'd lost her dream, and though she didn't want to admit it, she'd fallen in love with Dominic and lost him too. If she dwelled too much on all the bad things happening to her suddenly, she'd burst into tears.

Chapter Twenty-Five

Not wanting Diana to see him before he was ready, Dominic parked the Porsche behind the City Hall and walked across to the hotel. He whistled as he hopped onto the sidewalk. The change in his life since the last time he showed up in Cottage Grove was not lost on him.

He'd practically had to fight his way inside the double doors. The women had been crazy and determined in their quest to get a piece of him. Today, everyone left him alone and barely glanced at him. He had Diana to thank for the turnaround in his life.

Inside the old hotel, several people stood at the desk and a large group of individuals walked out of the restaurant to his left. He moved in closer and peered over the heads of the guests in front of him.

Diana stood with her head lowered, signing a paper behind the check-in desk, her curls loose and wild around her shoulders. She looked even more beautiful than he remembered.

He knew everything about Diana. He'd studied, mesmerized, and learned how fast she was to smile when he made her happy. She'd stand with her hand backward on her hip when he made her flustered. Most of all, he loved to watch her eyes ignite with passion and soften when he kissed her.

Diana tucked her hair behind her ear. He smiled, because at any moment he knew she'd brush the stray strand away from her face—yes, just like that. Now she'd bite her bottom lip. His grin stretched his cheeks. He'd missed her.

Diana moistened, and then raked her teeth over her bottom lip. His legs shook as her tongue tempted him to push his way through the crowd and kiss her.

Every movement, every breath she took, hypnotized him. How could he think that she'd walk away from him, feeling nothing or believing what they shared together was a fling? Stubborn and yet giving, she did what he expected her to do. Not what she wanted, because that's the type of person she was. He should've known.

He inhaled deeply, content to stand and watch her forever. But he had plans, and they needed to settle what was between them once and for all.

He'd never expected her to steal his jersey. That one simple act gave him hope that it wasn't too late.

He could fix letting her get on that plane and fly out of his life. All he had to do was convince her to listen.

"Excellent." Diana smiled at the couple in front of the desk. "Enjoy your stay."

She gazed out at the others in the group. He recognized the moment she spotted him, because she lost her smile.

"Hey, sweetcheeks," he mouthed.

She shook her head and frowned.

Burned from her reaction to seeing him, he peered around the room. Why wouldn't she be happy to see him?

"Excuse me." He shifted and walked between the guests, until he stood in front of the counter. "Diana, can I talk with you?"

"I'm working." She looked at the computer screen. "Unless you want a room, you'll have to leave."

He glanced over his shoulder. An older woman raised her brows and elbowed her husband, who jerked his gaze toward him and lifted his chin. He smiled politely and turned back around. "Yeah."

She snapped her gaze to him. "What?"

"I'd like to reserve a room at the hotel. For tonight." He reached behind him and extracted his wallet.

She blinked rapidly. "Dominic, you don't want to…"

"One night." He slid two hundred dollars across the counter. "Please."

She glared. "You don't want to stay here."

"Yes, I do," he said.

She stuck out her chin and challenged him. "No, you don't."

"Yes. I. Do." He grinned.

She leaned over the desk. "What are you doing here?" she hissed.

"Isn't it obvious? I want to talk with you."

"We've said all there is to say." She lowered her voice. "I'm not working for you any longer."

"Excuse me. How long is this going to take?" A man spoke behind him.

"It'll just be a minute." He winked at the man's wife and lifted his chin at the man in a silent plea for a few minutes of patience before turning back to Diana. "Have dinner with me."

She shook her head, stepped over to the printer, and slapped the paper down on the counter. "Sign."

He scribbled his name. "What time do you get off work?"

"I'm not going out to eat with you." She snatched the registration papers from him and tossed the key toward him.

"Chinese? Mexican?"

"Go away," she said.

"We'll order in, and—"

"No." She clamped her mouth shut, and peeked at the guests waiting their turn. "Don't you have a game to play?"

He grinned, because she was so damn cute when she tried to change the subject. "Suspended."

"That's not funny." She frowned. "What is wrong with you?"

"For once…nothing." He leaned over and braced his elbows on the counter. "Come closer to me."

"Why?" She shifted her gaze away from him.

He crooked his finger. "Come here."

She rolled her eyes and stepped toward the counter. "What?"

"A little bit closer," he whispered.

"Dom, this is ridiculous—" she leaned over the counter "—and not at all appropriate while I'm working."

"Who cares," he murmured, right before he kissed her.

For all his nonchalance and kidding, he went from slow to deep in a snap. All he could do was hold onto the counter to keep from hurdling over the top and showing her how damn much he missed her.

She met his tongue with her own. He deepened the kiss, excitement building in his chest until he felt like he could take on the whole Rangers team by himself in an away game. He slid his hand around her neck, keeping her from going away again. She stared into his eyes, questioning him without a word spoken.

"We need to talk," he whispered.

She rubbed her lips together. "No, we don't."

"Dinner? Please?"

"I'll be working through dinner," she said. "Leave a message on my phone if you want to talk to me."

"It's too important to tell you over the phone." He kissed her once more, fast and hard. "Dinner tonight. I'm not taking no for an answer. We'll talk, and then you'll understand."

He turned around. From behind him, she called, "Understand what?"

He waved over his shoulder, smiling. "You'll see, sweetcheeks."

Then not giving her a chance to deny him his wish, he strolled through the double doors and stepped out onto the sidewalk. He had no idea if she'd noticed the change in him or not but by tonight, she'd finally learn the truth.

Chapter Twenty-Six

Diana paced the small sitting area in her hotel room. It was seven o'clock. Dominic wasn't coming.

She'd ignored her excitement all day over seeing him again and soon learning why he'd come to Cottage Grove. When she wasn't glancing at the clock or peeking out the front door of the hotel, she beat herself up for how easily she fell back into thinking Dominic was her world. How could she expect him to be satisfied with a woman like her?

She'd failed in advancing her career when she missed purchasing the Ferriday house. He played professional hockey and traveled the world. She was stuck working for Mr. Dogger until she could make enough money to have a brand new bed & breakfast built. It'd take her years to supplement a loan of that size.

The phone rang. She rushed over, came to a careening stop, pressed her hand to her chest, and forced herself to cool down. She answered, calmer than she was feeling. "Hello?"

"Hey," Shauna said. "Do you have a cold?"

Her shoulders sagged. "No. Why?"

"You sound funny. All airy and depressed…have you been drinking?"

"Of course not." She rolled her eyes. "I'm fine."

"Yay. Good." Shauna laughed. "I'm picking you up in ten minutes. Wear something sexy and cute. Do you still have that pink sweater with the scooped neck you wore during the Valentine's dance at the hotel?"

"Yes, but I'm not—"

"Perfect! Wear a pair of ass fitting jeans and your black boots. Not too dressy, but casual hot." Diana's muffled voice came across the phone. "Sorry, Grayson came in the room, and I didn't want him to overhear me or he'd wonder what I was doing."

"Are you still denying him sex?"

Shauna snorted. "Are you kidding me? Grayson blew it. That man was all over me…but who can blame him, right?"

"Shauna…" Diana groaned. "Let's not talk about your late-blooming sex life tonight."

"Okay. Good plan, because tonight is all about you. Get ready, I'll be there soon, and I plan to show you the best time of your life. Whatever you do, don't leave your hotel room until I get there. Pinky swear?"

"Um, tonight isn't a good night, babe." She sank down in the chair. "That's what I've been trying to tell you. I've decided to stay in, take a bath, and…and do laundry."

Silence came over the line. Shauna cleared her throat. "I know Dominic's in town. He and Grayson are up to something, and I'm not going to let you keep beating yourself up over him. So get off your ass, get dressed, and be ready. No excuses."

The phone disconnected. Diana groaned and closed her eyes, clutching the phone to her chest. Dominic probably wanted to tell her he was in town to visit Grayson, and his being here had nothing to do with her. He didn't even show up after making a fool of her downstairs. She touched her lips. *Damn him.*

A voicemail would do for whatever he had to tell her. He didn't have to kiss her.

She opened her eyes and pulled herself out of the chair. Knowing Shauna, she'd be here before her ten minutes expired. She walked to the bedroom, dressed in the outfit Shauna picked out for her, and even put on her makeup.

By the time she pulled on her boots and decided she looked okay for whatever they were going to do, she'd worked up enough anger over Dominic not showing up, all she wanted to do was get out of the hotel and go somewhere to forget she ever fell in love with the big, sexy, Russian.

Knock, knock, knock.

She hurried into the sitting area, grabbed her purse, and opened the door. Shauna eyed her up and down, nodded, and pulled her out of the room. Diana locked the door, and, linking her arm through Shauna's, left the hotel.

A quarter a mile away, Shauna drove past Quayside Lounge. Diana frowned. "I thought you were taking me out for a drink."

"Change of plans," Shauna muttered.

She shifted in the passenger seat. "What are we doing?"

"You'll see," Shauna said.

"You're getting freaky again. The last time you acted secretive, I knew to expect a load of trouble coming your way." Diana nudged Shauna's arm. "I thought you said everything was okay between you and Grayson."

"Yeah. We're great." Shauna jolted. "Oh, turn the radio up. I love this song."

Diana shook her head, but turned the music louder. For the next mile, she let herself listen to the lyrics, wondering what Shauna heard in a song about breaking up when she had the ultimate love life. She, on the other hand, sunk further into a funk.

The car slowed down. She raised her gaze and frowned. "What are you doing here?"

"Don't ask." Shauna pulled into the driveway of the Ferriday house and came to a complete stop. "You know I love you, babe, but you need to get out of my car."

"W-what?" Her jaw dropped before anger consumed her. "I can't believe you," she whispered.

"Diana, I—"

She raised her hand. "Stop. You knew I lost my big chance, and you still brought me here. Why? I can't—" She clamped her lips shut and muffled her scream. "Never mind. I'll get out of the car, because I'll walk back to the hotel by myself."

"Diana!"

She slammed the car door. Behind her, she heard Shauna yell she was sorry. She whirled around and pointed. "Go!"

Standing in the driveway of someone else's pride and joy, and her broken dream, she watched Shauna back the car down the driveway and leave her behind. What in the world was Shauna thinking?

Never, in all the years they'd been friends, had Shauna been cruel or insensitive to her feelings. She kicked at the gravel on the driveway. There was no excuse for dumping her here. Even if she won the lottery, the house would still be unattainable to her. Gone. Never to be hers.

A hammering *bang, bang, bang* went off behind her. She whirled around. Shocked that someone would be out here at this time of night, she ducked behind the fence.

The windows on the bottom level of the Ferriday House were lit up and the noise came from inside. She brushed the tears from her eyes. All the times she'd walked through the house, she'd never viewed the house with the power on. For the first time in years, the place looked alive.

The serenity and majestic lay of the grand house took her breath away. How many times had she stood on the porch, looking out across the large span of yard and dreamed about turning the place into the best bed and breakfast in the county?

A shadow walked by the window. She crept closer, being quiet in case whoever was inside caught her trespassing. One little peek, that's all, and then she'd leave. She had to see what the inside looked like with all the lights chasing away the dust and cobwebs.

The porch step creaked when she took her first step. She froze, watching the door. In the night, she could've sworn the sound echoed.

Before she could advance to the window, the door opened. A large darkened form filled the doorway, the inside lights casting his face in shadows. She gasped. Only one man could make that big of a silhouette.

"What are you doing here?" She stepped up on the porch.

Dominic moved back inside in the light. "I want to show you something. Come in."

In one day, he'd changed from his slacks and a dress shirt from this morning into an old pair of jeans with a frayed rip on the thigh, faded spots on his knees, and a worn T-shirt. His mussed hair held up a pair of safety goggles. Her gaze went back down his body to the tool belt buckled low on his hips. She blinked at the hammer in his hand.

"Oh my freaking God. Are you crazy?" She stomped into the house. "You can't break into this house. Someone bought it."

"I know," he said. "I'm only tearing something apart."

She threw her hands up to her sides. "You are—" She clamped her lips together and shook her head. "So freaking in trouble. Stop doing whatever you are doing and get out of here."

She hated the way her voice broke and the way she showed how much seeing him here hurt. Sure, he was Dominic Chekovsky, famous hockey player, but he couldn't do whatever he wanted. Cottage Grove police would throw him in jail for breaking and entering. Not to mention destroying a perfectly spectacular historical home.

"Follow me." He motioned with his hand and walked into the kitchen.

She didn't want to. She wanted to get out of here before someone caught them. But she couldn't stop herself from absorbing everything about the entryway with the old chandelier glowing. The crown molding, a highlight of the original woodwork, only needed sanding and polishing.

In the living room, she scanned the long sectional wooden floor. She'd always assumed she'd need to have a new floor built, but the wood planks were gorgeous. She ran her hand across her cheek. God, she would've loved to varnish the floors to a shine. The history they told with their age would attract all the guests' attention during their stay.

She stepped into the kitchen and her heart dropped. "Oh my God, what have you done?"

"I ripped out the old stove and cabinet. It's in the backyard." He moved over to the fireplace. "Did you know the chimney's still intact and seems in good condition?"

Of course she did. She'd dug up every piece of information she could find on the house. She'd spent numerous hours being nosey, scouring the property, doing research in the library. She knew the cellar door on the outside remained broken, and the foundation on the east corner needed fixing, but the beams under the house were solid and in good condition. At one time, there was a winery in the backyard, but had since been torn down. Nothing he told her now would surprise her.

Except why he was standing in the house pretending he had permission to rip apart the kitchen.

"Dom...you're killing me," she whispered.

He approached her and took her hands in his. "We need to talk."

"There's nothing to say. I did my part for you. Someone else bought this house. I'm working at the hotel until I can make other plans." She lifted her gaze. "And you have a hockey career you must take seriously. If you are caught vandalizing this house, you can kiss everything goodbye. We need to leave. Now."

He shook his head. "I have a bigger problem."

Despite telling herself he was none of her business, she asked, "What?"

"You failed to do what I hired you for." He lifted her hands and kissed her knuckles.

She cringed. "The women are bothering you again?"

"No." He chuckled. "They ignore me."

She tugged on her hands, but he refused to let her go. "Well, I'm sorry that disappoints you. I'm sure you can do whatever you do and have them back."

"I don't want them," he whispered. "I want you. You see, I realized that having you around all the time wasn't what made them stay away from me. I didn't need your protection."

Kill me now. She glared. "Fine. I guess you're here to ask for your money back. You're too late. I tore the check in half and mailed it to your house already. I don't want your money, and seeing how you don't think I did my job, we can both be happy."

"I didn't say I wasn't happy." His jaw twitched. "I said it wasn't you who made all the women stop chasing me. I did that."

"God. You are a conceited ass—"

"They stopped throwing themselves at me because I fell in love with you." He pressed her hands to his chest and held them there. "In my heart, I was taken the moment you came home with me. When you are around, all I can see is you. I went to bed thinking about you, and woke up anxious to be with you. Nothing else exists. The women, they know I'll never see anything in them because you are my everything."

Okay. That was perfect.

"I am?" she mouthed.

He leaned forward and put his lips to her ear. "You are, sweetcheeks," he whispered.

"Oh my God." She pulled her hands out of his grasp and dived into his arms. "I fell in love with you too. I wanted to tell you, but I thought you only hired me to do a job. Then I didn't think I deserved you, because I whored myself out to you and you were not the player I thought you were."

"It was never a job. The first time I saw you, I wanted you." He tilted her face. "I love you."

"I love you, too," she said.

He kissed her. There were no words to describe what they said with their lips. Her confession topped with finally having her mouth on him again was soul shattering and thorough. Deep and hypnotic. It was better than anything she'd ever dreamed.

His mouth was the perfect mold for her lips. His tongue tangled with hers. He held her still, wanting her to accept him, and she did without any question.

There was nothing but him and her. And the feelings they finally let out into the open.

Nothing compared to their kiss. Nothing. Not her independence or her broken dreams. Not his pushy ways or his career or even all the women he came into contact with on a daily basis. Not any of the hurdles she knew they'd need to jump would keep her from Dominic again.

When he lifted his head a fraction of an inch, he placed his forehead against hers. She breathed deep, feeling the tingles on her sensitized lips after the kiss and knew he felt it too.

Finally, he spoke. "Diana, will you—"

A loud roar of cars grew close to the house, followed by slamming doors, pulling them apart. She gaped at Dom before jumping into action.

"Run!" She grabbed his sleeve and pulled.

He caught her around the waist. "Diana, it's okay."

"No, it's not. This is Cottage Grove. Being a hockey player won't get you out of being charged with trespassing and damaging someone else's property." She kicked out when he lifted her off the ground. "I don't want to go to jail."

The front door banged open. She stilled in Dominic's arms as footsteps pounded over the wooden floor growing closer.

Shauna skidded to a stop in the kitchen. "I'm so sorry, Diana. Don't be mad. It's Grayson's fault. He wouldn't tell me what was going on, but I overheard him talking to Dominic at the tennis center and I couldn't let—"

Grayson appeared behind Shauna and covered her mouth with his hand. "Sorry, you two. She slipped away from me."

Diana sagged in relief and smiled at Shauna. Everything about tonight made more sense now that Dominic had confessed his love to her. "It's okay."

Shauna squealed behind Grayson's hand and gave her two thumbs up. Diana laughed, leaning into Dominic. God, she loved her friends. Their friends.

"We'll be going now," Grayson mumbled, picking Shauna up and packing her out of the house.

When the door closed, Diana turned to Dominic. "We really do need to leave. The house isn't for sale anymore. Someone bought it before I could put an offer down."

"Just a moment." He took a deep breath. "I can't spend another day without you. I know we have a lot to figure out, but the possibilities of spending the rest of my life with you and figuring all this out as we go makes me feel alive." He paused, and sucked more air into his chest. "Diana, will you marry me?"

She covered her mouth. Moisture blurred her vision.

"Sweetcheeks…?"

She nodded. Tears leaked through her eyelashes and spilled down her cheeks as she answered him.

Dominic laughed. "I have no idea what you said. You'll have to move your hand off your mouth."

She removed her hand and jumped into his arms. Against his neck, she chanted, "Yes, yes, yes, yes."

He carried her as he kissed her all over her face. Her butt hit a flat surface and she pulled back, seeing he'd put her on the counter by the sink. She ran her hands over his gorgeous face, unable to believe he loved her as much as she loved him.

She grinned, shimmying on the old, dusty counter. "We're getting married."

"I've been busy the last several days, and haven't had time to buy you a ring," he said, taking off his tool belt.

She shook her head. "It doesn't matter. We have time."

"That's not good enough for my girl." He dug in his back pocket. "So I thought maybe this would make it easier to wait until we can both go in together and pick out a ring."

She tilted her head and took the piece of paper from him. "What is it?"

"Read it," he said.

She unfolded the paper, rubbed her eyes, and bent her head forward. After reading the first line, she gasped.

"I couldn't let your dream slip away," he whispered. "You've worked too hard. The Ferriday house is yours. Free and clear. On one condition..."

She pressed the paper to her chest. "What?"

"You give my jersey back to me that you stole." He kissed her hard. "Then you wear it every night in my bed."

She wrapped herself around him and planted her head in his neck. Life, at that moment, was perfect. She put her lips to his ear and whispered, "You've got deal, big guy. I love you."

About the Author

Top Selling Romance Author, Debra Kayn, lives with her family in the beautiful coastal mountains of Oregon on a hobby farm. She enjoys riding motorcycles, gardening, playing tennis, and fishing. A huge animal lover, she always has a dog under her desk when she writes and chickens standing at the front door looking for a treat. She's famous in her family for teaching a 270 pound hog named Harley to jog with her every morning.

Her love of family ties and laughter makes her a natural to write heartwarming contemporary stories to the delight of her readers. Oh, let's cut to the chase. She loves to write about *REAL MEN* and the *WOMEN* who love them.

When Debra was nineteen years old, a man kissed her without introducing himself. When they finally came up for air, the first words out of his mouth were…will you have my babies? Considering Debra's weakness for a sexy, badass man who is strong enough to survive her attitude, she said yes. A quick wedding at the House of Amour and four babies later, she's living her own romance book.

www.debrakayn.com
www.twitter.com/DebraKayn
www.facebook.com/DebraKaynFanPage

More from This Author

(From *Wildly*)

Shauna Marino walked toward the front door of Schyler Tennis Center—or straight to hell—she wouldn't know for sure until she stood before Grayson Schyler with her heart in her hand. With a toss of her hair and a fortifying breath, she forced herself to take the last remaining steps to face her past. If she'd planned the epic occasion better, she would've brought a bottle of tequila along to soften the outcome.

The wind caught the outer door and slammed it shut behind her with an ominous *whoosh*. She flinched, and then tried to hide her shaky reaction of being back in Grayson's territory by wiping the palm of her hand on the front of her white tennis skirt. She hadn't seen him in over six years, but the same anxiety-excitement-fear emotional cocktail threatened her resolve to pull this meeting off with class and calmness.

She inspected the front of her light pink, sleeveless polo shirt and flicked at an imaginary piece of lint. The odds were good that Grayson wouldn't even recognize her. Not at first, anyway.

No longer the innocent teenager, gangly and wilder than the coastal winds, always diving headfirst into whatever feelings ruled the moment, she hoped to rekindle her friendship with Grayson. Before she could show him how much she'd changed though, she'd have to prove she'd left her old ways behind her.

"Hi. Can I help you?" To the right of the door, a young man behind the front desk stood up from his perch at the computer and approached the counter.

"I have a lesson with Grayson at eleven. My name's Shauna." She stared straight ahead, her heart beating wildly in her chest.

When she'd called and made the appointment, she'd left only her first name—spelled the wrong way to be on the safe side. The idea to keep Grayson in the dark about her return had seemed brilliant at the time. She didn't want him reminded of how she'd made a complete fool of herself all through high school with her wild crush on him. She hoped the element of surprise would be enough to knock him speechless when they finally did come face to face.

Maybe then she would be able to utter the two words she should've said years ago. *I'm sorry.*

She looked up at the oversized poster of Grayson holding the Wimbledon trophy. Warmth beat out the nervousness inside her stomach, and she leaned forward. She'd never missed one of Grayson's matches on television, or an opportunity to be with him back when she'd still lived at home. It seemed like her whole life revolved around loving Grayson.

He'd started out as her idol when she was twelve years old and he was nineteen. Then, during the winters, when he came home in the off-season to teach at the tennis center, she'd used whatever creative act she could think up to spend time with him. Despite their age difference, they'd become friends. He'd fascinated her with his world travels, his responsibilities, and his goals. He was the young man who thought she was a funny kid, and she'd done whatever possible to make him laugh.

Shauna caught herself tapping the counter with her fingernail and stopped.

Looking back, she knew she'd gone overboard more often than naught, much to the disgrace of the town. But she could also point out that she and Grayson had supported each other while they'd dealt with their own individual hurts. They'd connected on a level that exceeded the normal friendships that came and went. She rubbed her arm. He'd meant everything to her. Smart, ambitious, and compassionate, he'd shown her that someone cared about her.

It wasn't until she'd turned sixteen that her world spiraled out of control, and she'd fallen head over heels in love with Grayson. She no longer saw him as her mentor, her coach, and she couldn't accept why he'd suddenly pushed her away and left their friendship behind.

For two years, she'd gone to the extreme to reconnect with him, much to his anger. Finally, on her eighteenth birthday, she'd had enough. She was an adult, and he could no longer tell her she was a child and to stay away.

She'd shown up at his office with only her long coat covering her naked body. She swallowed at remembering how his eyes flared as she'd explained why she'd come to him. The intensity in which he'd jerked the edges of her coat closed, turned her around, and pushed her out the door devastated her.

After that, he had nothing to do with her and she'd finally accepted that she'd lost her best friend. On that horrible day when she'd decided to give everything to Grayson, her dad met her on the front porch when she'd arrived home, rejected, hurting, and broken. Grayson had ratted her out, and she was in trouble. Her stomach flipped and she inhaled deeply. Not long after, her father claimed to have had enough of her shenanigans and sent her away to college to grow up.

She'd done her best to move on with her life, and experience more of the world while attending Cal State, to forget about her past. She'd excelled in school, made friends, and a new life for herself. But, the time had come to return to where she'd grown up and repair her reputation. "Are you a registered member here?" the clerk asked.

She shook her head. "No. A guest."

At one time, she'd spent every day improving her game under the guise of being close to Grayson, but she'd dropped her membership and the sport completely when her dad surprised her and sent her to Cal State. She spun the handle of her graphite racket. Away from home, she'd waited for her feelings to change, but instead her feelings for Grayson had grown stronger.

"That'll be thirty-five dollars." The man held out his hand, and proceeded to scan her debit card before handing it back to her. "Grayson will be finishing his lesson in—" he looked up at the clock "—five minutes. Go ahead and go through the double doors behind you. You'll be playing on the clay court. If you want to warm up now, you'll be all ready when he's done. If you need anything else, my name's Daniel."

"Thank you, Daniel." She kept to the right of the counter, crossed the large lobby where onlookers gathered to observe the three indoor courts, and pushed through the double doors leading to the play area. Back to back, the grass, concrete, and clay surfaces provided every player the opportunity to practice on different playing fields.

She dawdled behind the ceiling-to-floor curtain used to block off the pathway behind the courts from flying tennis balls. She peeked between the openings of the fabric to the first court. What would one little look hurt?

Six feet away, Grayson stood with his back to her. Her stomach fluttered. All smooth, firm lines of his six-foot killer body, so close, so touchable, so out of her league. He hadn't changed a bit.

He still wore his sandy brown hair longer than most guys did, the ends only beginning to curl as they skimmed the collar of his T-shirt. His broad shoulders bunched and bulged beneath his shirt. His strong arm swung the racket in a smooth arch, showing his raw talent for the sport.

She held her breath, afraid he'd sense her behind him. Her gaze lowered to the white tennis shorts hugging his muscular ass and pulling tighter every time he moved his legs. Solid legs that left her clenching the curtain in her hand for support. Legs she would've recognized anywhere.

"Last set, Jason. Let's make each stroke count." Grayson reached into his pocket and pulled out a tennis ball, effortlessly sailing it over the net with the ease of a lifetime of practice. "Follow through…"

Shauna dropped the curtain, panting. *Oh my God. What am I doing?*

She hurried down the aisle to the appointed court and jogged out into the playing area. Keeping her back to the other players on the grass court, she raised the racket above her head with both hands and leaned to the side, stretching her back. Then she bounced on her toes and warmed up her leg muscles. At best, she hoped to muster up enough skill to play a decent game and hit the ball over the net.

If Grayson were willing to see past their history, if she could convince him she'd matured, if she proved her worth, maybe he'd believe that she'd returned a changed woman. She caught herself clutching the end of her skirt, and quickly rubbed any possible wrinkles out of the material. If she could step back into the community and erase her reputation as the wild girl of Cottage Grove, her life would finally get back on track from when she'd derailed at twelve years old.

She wasn't coming back as Tony Marino's daughter, or the child whose mother had abandoned her, or Grayson's biggest pain in the ass.

Shauna would never live down all the embarrassing things she did in the name of love as a teenager. Trailing Grayson around town, telling everyone who would listen how much she loved him, leaving him gifts, even throwing herself at him, only to be turned down cold in the end. And all through it, the whole town was laughing at her, the wild child who was obsessed with the town's golden boy.

No, she had a much more important job to do.

Two weeks ago, the city of Cottage Grove had hired her to head the Chamber of Commerce. She had plans, and if it were the last thing she tried to do, she'd impress everyone. And, maybe then, she could let go of all her guilt.

If she failed to prove she wasn't going to hurt Grayson now that she was back, then she'd have to figure out a way to move on with the black cloud hovering over her. Granted it would be with a broken heart, but she'd survive. She always did.

Out of her peripheral vision, the curtain parted. She lowered her arms and faced her lifelong love with the grace of someone who knew exactly what she wanted, terrified she'd screw up once again. *I can do this. I've changed. I'm strong. I'm mature. I'm…such a goner.*

"Shauna?" Grayson held out his hand. "I'm your instructor, Grayson."

She pried her tongue off the roof of her mouth and met his gaze while reaching for the handshake. If she accomplished anything, she hoped it was the ability to keep her game face on for the next hour. "Hello, Grayson."

In the mood for more Crimson Romance?
Check out *Georgie's Heart*
by Kathryn Brocato
at *CrimsonRomance.com.*